"I keep my
possible c

Mark couldn't take his eyes from Leah's face. His heart had swelled, and he understood what all the emotions rushing through him meant.

This woman was perfect for him. She formed with some inner picture inside him of what the mother of his child—what his partner in life—should be.

"I think I'm falling in love with you," he said.

She flushed, the color doubling on her high cheekbones. "You think that because I'm carrying your child."

Dear Reader,

Welcome back to THE STATE OF PARENTHOOD miniseries, Harlequin American Romance's celebration of parenthood and place. In this, our twenty-fifth year of publishing great books, we're delighted to bring you these heartwarming stories that sing the praises of the home state of six different authors, and share the many trials and delights of being a parent.

In *Holding the Baby*, set in a small Colorado town, Margot Early looks at an unconventional family situation. Leah Williams is carrying a child for her sister, who decides she will not take the baby after all, leaving Leah with an unexpected, lifelong commitment. Mark Logan, the sperm donor and biological father, wants to be involved in the baby's life—effectively bringing two total strangers together. A baby is a miracle in itself—but falling in love because of a child is something even more wondrous and beautiful.

There are five other books in this series: Tina Leonard's *Texas Lullaby* (June '08), *Smoky Mountain Reunion* by Lynnette Kent (July '08), *Cowboy Dad* by Cathy McDavid (August '08) or *A Dad for Her Twins* by Tanya Michaels (September '08). Next month watch for our final book, *A Daddy for Christmas* by Laura Marie Altom, when we head west to Oklahoma for a heartwarming holiday story.

We hope these romantic stories inspire you to celebrate where you live—because any place you raise a child is home.

Wishing you happy reading,

Kathleen Scheibling
Senior Editor
Harlequin American Romance

Holding the Baby
Margot Early

TORONTO • NEW YORK • LONDON
AMSTERDAM • PARIS • SYDNEY • HAMBURG
STOCKHOLM • ATHENS • TOKYO • MILAN • MADRID
PRAGUE • WARSAW • BUDAPEST • AUCKLAND

ISBN-13: 978-0-373-75233-1
ISBN-10:   0-373-75233-4

HOLDING THE BABY

ABOUT THE AUTHOR

Margot Early has written stories since she was twelve
years old. She has sold 3,600,000 books published
with Harlequin; her work has been translated into
nine languages and sold in sixteen countries. Ms. Early
lives high in Colorado's San Juan Mountains with two
German shepherds and several other pets, including
snakes and tarantulas. She enjoys the outdoors, dance
and spinning dog hair.

Books by Margot Early

HARLEQUIN SUPERROMANCE

766—WHO'S AFRAID OF THE MISTLETOE?
802—YOU WERE ON MY MIND
855—TALKING ABOUT MY BABY
878—THERE IS A SEASON
912—FOREVER AND A BABY
1333—HOW TO GET MARRIED
1357—A FAMILY RESEMBLANCE
1376—WHERE WE WERE BORN
1401—BECAUSE OF OUR CHILD
1436—GOOD WITH CHILDREN

HARLEQUIN EVERLASTING LOVE

3—THE DEPTH OF LOVE
22—A SPIRIT OF CHRISTMAS

For Maureen with love

Chapter One

Paonia, Colorado

"I'm pregnant," Ellen announced gleefully.

"You're what?" Not the reaction Ellen was probably looking for, Leah Williams thought. That her younger sister, thirty-two, happily married for six years, was carrying a longed-for child should have been great news. As it was, Leah absently poured orange juice, intended for four-year-old Mary Grace's cup, into her bowl of muesli.

"Mom!"

"Oh, sh— Sorry. I'll eat it. Maybe I can pour it... Darling, just a minute."

The life inside Leah's abdomen gave a kick, as if the baby could sense the turmoil Ellen's words caused.

"So we'll be pregnant together," Ellen continued, "and we'll have new babies at about the same time. Mine's due December first. I think. Anyhow, our kids will be cousins and really close in age...."

I never planned on keeping this baby. This was your baby, Ellen.

"Ellen, hang on. I need to deal with cereal." She put down the phone. Ellen was pregnant. How was Ellen pregnant? And what was supposed to happen to the baby—Ellen's baby, for crying out loud—that Leah was carrying? Of course, Ellen had made her wishes clear—Leah would keep the baby.

She picked up the phone and said, "Mary Grace, I'm going in the other room for a minute."

Her daughter, who had Sam's hay-colored hair and Leah's dark eyes, nodded without looking up from her bowl. She ate with deliberation, as she did everything.

Leah stared out the window. The two acres of peach orchards on which the small historic farmhouse sat had been Sam's promised land. Leah loved the little three-bedroom house, loved to gaze out over the fertile valley at the snow-draped mountains.

Stifling a sigh, she put the phone to her ear.

First things first. Though she wasn't sure what should come first.

She spoke to her sister. "You're thinking…I'll just keep this baby."

"Well, it's up to you," Ellen said. "But I thought you'd want to."

Leah walked back over to the windows that fronted the tiny living room. Gazing out at mountains far to the north, she asked, "How did you come to be pregnant?"

Ellen's husband, River, was a Desert Storm veteran. After leaving the military, he'd changed his name and taken up organic farming. Then, he'd met Ellen, and ever since they'd been trying for a pregnancy. After more than three years and no baby, they'd figured that they were, as a couple, infertile, and, unwilling to go to a fertility clinic, they'd asked Leah to have a child for them, the sperm to be provided by River's half brother, Mark.

Leah had drawn the line at conceiving a baby the natural way with Mark Logan!

River and Ellen, talked through every step of the process and reassured that no fertility drugs, for instance, would be used, had finally agreed that artificial insemination could take place in the office of a nearby Delta midwife, Kassandra Warner.

"You're pregnant," Leah repeated. "With River's child."

"Yes. Of course." Ellen paused. "You *will* be our midwife, won't you?"

"Yes," said Leah. She was ready to put down the phone and be alone and think—or maybe just scream. Granted, Ellen hadn't *planned* this. Ellen and River had believed that they couldn't conceive a child together. Nonetheless, the situation seemed so *typical.* Ellen was flighty and unreliable, and Leah had allowed herself to be persuaded to conceive and carry a child to give to her sister and River, and now this.

She had to get off the phone. But there was still one question to ask, because the child she carried... Well, the baby had another biological parent. "Does Mark know?"

A pause. "I hadn't thought to let him know. I guess I should, because River and I won't be the parents of

your baby. You will be. I'll call him. Right now. Go
back to Mary Grace."

Click.

Leah sank onto an antique love seat by the window.
Once again her gaze was drawn to the distant mountains. Mark Logan.

She'd known him for years, though just as an ac-
quaintance. Women throughout the San Juan Mountains and north along Colorado's western slope swore
he was like a brother to them, that he was the best guy
there was. Men respected him. And everyone agreed
that he was the most capable mountaineer and backcountry guide in the area.

Leah found him abrasive. For whatever reason,
she'd never felt comfortable in his presence. In any
case, he'd never tried to secure her good opinion. He
had been Ellen's choice as a father for the child Leah
now carried. Ellen's and River's. Leah definitely
would have picked someone else. But she'd gone
along with the baby project because Ellen and River
had been desperate, and Leah had wanted to give this
gift to her sister.

Well, it could be worse. Mark could come to Paonia
and fight her over this child. Luckily for her, that wasn't
going to happen. After having donated sperm to this
project, he'd returned to his mountain home and hadn't
looked back. He would leave the hard decisions to her.

Now, she must make them.

"LEAH?" She'd already seen by the caller ID that the
call was coming from Mark Logan's cell phone. So the

deep, slightly gravelly voice should have been no surprise.

"Yes." She couldn't work up any friendliness, hadn't yet recovered from Ellen's announcement. Obviously, Ellen had wasted no time getting hold of him.

"You and I need to talk. I'll be down there by five-thirty. I'll take you to dinner. Can you get a sitter?"

This was what she so disliked about the man. He hadn't asked if she was free. He hadn't asked if she had money for a sitter. He'd just tried to take charge. Well, he could be as dictatorial as he liked, but it wasn't going to work with her. "No. I can't get a sitter. You can have dinner and come to the house after Mary Grace is asleep. Eight-thirty will be fine."

Silence. Then, "Okay. Can I pick anything up for you on the way?"

"No, thank you."

"I'll see you then."

Click.

Businesslike.

"Baby," Leah said as she studied herself in the mirror, "it's you and me."

She smoothed a hand over her belly, admiring her maternity clothes. They'd been made by a Paonia designer, actually sewn in Paonia as well, and her red flared pants and matching tunic at once slimmed and emphasized the beauty of pregnancy.

She considered whether to wear her hair up or down and finally settled on a single braid down her back.

Mary Grace came into the room, carrying one of her

stuffed animals, a unicorn named Secret. Unlike several of Mary Grace's other animals, Secret did not talk. He could keep a secret.

"You look pretty, Mommy."

"You are always pretty," she told her daughter.

Now is the time, she thought. She'd had hours to come to terms with the idea of the baby being her child instead of Ellen's. Now she had to break the news to Mary Grace.

"Ellen doesn't want our baby?" Mary Grace asked, after Leah had tried to explain what was happening.

"It's not that she doesn't want our baby. But she's having one of her own. So I'm going to have this baby, and you will have a brother or sister."

Mary Grace frowned thoughtfully. "This way is better," she said. "It makes more sense."

Having a mother who was a midwife, sometimes being taken to births in the middle of the night, Mary Grace had a strange maturity. She gave off a sense of knowing and wisdom. Leah found her daughter to be wholly remarkable and hoped the baby she was carrying would be as easy as Mary Grace had always been.

This is crazy. I did not plan to have a baby myself.

She said, "What story tonight?"

LEAH HEARD his vehicle pull up on the dirt drive. She opened the front door and watched him come up the walk, his blond hair a bright spot under the stars.

Mark's blue eyes took in her appearance in one sweeping glance—then he seemed to dismiss her.

She stepped back, holding the door open, and he

came in, giving the foyer with its old-fashioned wainscoting the same sort of look he'd given her. She shut the door and led him into the living room. Her furniture was lodgepole pine, most of it crafted by Sam. Sam had been able to do so many things, and Leah had loved him. But his sudden death hadn't caused unending grief so much as a sense of being overwhelmed, of needing to swim, swim, swim to keep her head above water.

The weighted windows were shaded now by blinds designed for energy efficiency, and they were keeping the house warm against the chill March night. Summer would be here soon, summer which meant more work in the garden and longer days with Mary Grace by her side and trips to the river and the swimming pond.

How am I going to earn enough to support two children?

She gestured Mark toward the couch. "Can I get you anything? Water? Tea?" She had beer in the fridge—primarily for River when he and Ellen came over—but felt disinclined to offer it. This was simple nastiness on her part. It wasn't his fault that Ellen and River had so unexpectedly conceived a child. "Beer?" she finally said, relenting.

"Water would be great. Thank you."

She went to the kitchen and poured one for him and one for herself. Stalling for time, she took half a lemon from the refrigerator and garnished each glass with a slice. Added ice. She returned to the living room, handed Mark one of the glasses and sat down in the rocking chair at one end of the couch.

He drove straight to the matter at hand. "We need to decide what to do. You live here. My work is in the San Juans." He was a backcountry tour guide who operated a chain of huts through the mountains. "There will be a lot of traveling back and forth in order for us to share custody, but obviously that's what needs to happen."

Leah was momentarily dumbstruck. Then, she gave a brief, raw laugh. *"Obviously?"*

"You and I have conceived a child," he said in that same matter-of-fact, knows-what-is-best-for-everyone way. "I don't expect you to raise our child on your own."

"I could put the child up for adoption." Leah could not bring herself to say "our" and thought it wrong to say "my." In any case, she had no intention of putting the baby up for adoption, but she wanted to hear his reaction to the possibility.

"I wouldn't go along with that," he said.

"I'm not sure you have any choice in the matter." Who did he think he was?

"Let's say that I would prefer to keep better track of my sperm."

"I like that word. *Prefer,*" she emphasized.

His smile didn't reach his eyes. "My *preferred* plan for the child you are carrying is that you and I share in its future."

"I have a child already," she said, "and we're doing just fine without help." She blocked out memories of the months after Sam's accident, of the shock of discovering she was alone in the world, that she was a single parent, which she'd never planned to be.

In the hours since Ellen had announced her pregnancy, Leah had imagined many scenarios involving the baby she herself carried. None of those scenarios had involved Mark Logan.

Now, despite the discouragement she couldn't help giving, part of her felt shame that she had so discounted him. Did she believe she could do a better job raising the child alone without the father's input?

But I don't like this man.

That didn't necessarily mean he would be a lousy father. If she meant to keep the baby, she should at least welcome this man's willingness to be part of the child's life.

Mark studied her and drank his water. Leah Williams was beautiful, no doubt about it. He was curious to see what the child they'd conceived would look like. Would their baby have her dark auburn hair and brown eyes? Or would it take after him? Ellen's and River's announcement had more than irritated him. He hadn't donated his sperm lightly. He had counted on them to raise the child.

It had occurred to him that she might want to give the baby up for adoption. He'd been prepared to take over as a single father rather than let her do that. He just didn't like the idea of having a child out there and not knowing what had become of the life that was part of him.

He said, "If you want to give the child up for adoption, I am willing to take the baby."

"Rather than see him—or her—go to a home with two parents?"

She was toying with him. She must be. He decided to let her play out all her rope. "Yes."

Abruptly, she said, "I'm keeping this baby."

"Excellent."

"And I'm glad you want to be an active father." This, Leah knew, was very close to a lie.

"Then, that's settled," he said. "And you can count on my paying child support as well."

"I suppose," she said with a visible lack of enthusiasm, "you may attend the birth. In fact, it would be my preference that you do."

"I will."

He smiled suddenly, transforming his face from hard and forbidding to... Well, Leah's stomach flooded with warmth. "I'm excited," he said. "I didn't plan on this happening, but I'm glad to have another child."

"Another?" He was divorced, she knew. Her heart quivered oddly. Every nerve in her body seemed to come alive at his words—his assertion that he wanted this child. Must be the hormones.

"I have a daughter. Camille. She's sixteen. She lives with her mother in California. As for this baby, there's still the problem," he said, "that we live in different communities. I don't expect the baby to be separated from you fifty percent of the time while you're nursing."

Fifty percent? "You have joint custody of your daughter?" Leah asked.

"No." Bitterness crept into the single word. "We had a fairly serious custody battle, and Sabrina won. I get eight weeks a year visitation and may speak to her on the phone once a week."

Leah gazed at him in surprise. "Why so little time?"

"A few reasons. My home was up in the mountains and off the grid, and the judge seemed to think that wasn't a suitable sort of environment for a young girl. So I bought a place in Ouray with an upstairs apartment. I lived there during the custody battle. Camille attended day care in Ouray. Sabrina talked a lot about advantages she could offer Camille in California."

"It still doesn't seem fair. What did the home study say?"

A moment's hesitation. "The psychologist felt I had an authoritarian personality. The judge also felt that it weighted heavily that Camille is a girl— thought she should be with her mother. And she was very young. Three."

Leah took all this in—well imagining why a psychologist might think an authoritarian father wasn't the best primary custodian for a three-year-old girl. She returned to the topic of the child she was carrying. "I don't intend to leave Paonia," she said. "This is a good place for me. I have a backup physician who is supportive of my home-birth practice."

Mark heard her. But what could he do in Paonia? His life was the mountains. He was a guide, a business owner. He had some money put away, but he enjoyed work, needed to work. Paonia was a new-age farming community, a place to grow things. If he were to move here—and that was premature—he'd need a job.

"What are you thinking?" she asked.

"Just trying to work out the problems. I can't walk away from my business just now, but I'll want to be near the baby."

"And I certainly can't leave *my* business," she reiterated. "People depend on me."

"Yes." Pregnant women. He and Leah both took care of other lives. For him, that happened in the mountains. For her, it was pregnant women, mothers and infants.

"Well, we've settled some things at least," Leah said. "Maybe we should leave it at that for now. If you want to figure out how you can move to Paonia, be my guest. But my course for the next few months will be the same as if Ellen was going to be the baby's mother."

"You would have been able to give up the baby." The statement was a question.

"Well—yes. I'd planned to. I never considered this baby as mine until—" Until a few hours ago. And ever since, she had thought of the baby as hers.

He said, "I'd like to spend some time with both you and Mary Grace." He had seen Leah's daughter a few times at River and Ellen's but hadn't interacted with her. He told Leah, "In fact, I have an idea. I'd like you and Mary Grace to take a weekend trip into the mountains with me."

"Why?" Leah asked suspiciously.

"To get to know you," Mark said.

When she didn't say anything, he asked, "You don't want to?"

"It's not that." From the moment he'd shown up at her door he'd been assessing and judging her. Deep down, she suspected that he'd invited her and Mary Grace on this trip so he could to observe her mothering skills.

He asked, "Do you have to be available to your clients all the time?"

"I would if I had clients expecting babies soon. The doctor covers for me. But I'm not really a mountaineering type." Despite her misgivings about Mark, she was intrigued by the idea of a mountain trip. "I don't ski or anything."

"We can go on snowshoes. Or by dog sled."

"Are you a musher?"

"A couple runs trips for me. They have twenty-seven dogs at last count."

"Oh." Going off into the mountains on a dog sled sounded wildly—well, romantic. Mary Grace would love it. "How much do you charge for those trips?"

"Come on," he said with a laugh. "I'm the owner."

"I want to know though."

"Five hundred dollars a day."

Her eyes widened. His job paid better than midwifery. Of course, the couple with the dogs must get a good bit of the fee. "All right. We'll go for a dog-sled trip with you," she decided abruptly.

"You'd be okay?" he asked.

"Why wouldn't I?"

"You're pregnant."

She expelled a breath. "It's not a sickness."

He laughed. "Okay. Let's look at a calendar and pick a date."

Leah stood, and her legs were watery-weak, and tremors ran through her which she hoped did not show. She went to the wall calendar where she kept track of appointments, took it down from the wall and brought it to Mark.

"Peace," he said, because that was the theme of the

calendar, with colorful photos of peace marches and works of art promoting peace. Again his handsome smile, a half smile this time.

They selected a weekend two weeks ahead.

The phone rang, and Leah stood to answer it.

Ellen. "Hi. I've been sick all day. How long does this last?"

"Probably not a very long time," Leah said. She knew women who'd had morning sickness for the better part of their pregnancies, but this was the exception and she wasn't about to tell her sister of that possibility. Instead, she recommended protein and vitamin B6. "Are you taking a prenatal vitamin?"

"I wanted to ask you which ones are the cleanest."

Yes, for Ellen's vegan diet, for her beliefs about taking anything in pill form, this would be an issue.

"Look, let's talk later. Someone's here right now."

"Who?"

Leah felt reluctant to tell her. "Mark."

A pause. "Mark who?"

Again, Leah experienced amazement at her sister's thoughtlessness. "Your husband's brother. Your brother-in-law. The Mark whose child I'm carrying." Then, she wished she hadn't used those words in front of him. His child.

When she'd gotten off the phone, she found him watching her.

His eyes mirrored her own reaction to Ellen's and River's recent decisions.

"This isn't what you'd planned, is it?" he said unnecessarily.

"Well—" Leah hesitated before answering fully. "I suppose being a midwife has taught me that things don't always happen according to plan—our plans, that is."

Mark smiled again, a tad rueful. "Isn't that the truth." He rose from the couch and said, "That being the case, I'll nonetheless plan to see you and Mary Grace in Ouray in two weeks. Call and let me know if you need anything, anything at all. You're all right for money?"

"Yes." She certainly wasn't going to begin taking his money at this point. She lived carefully—always had even before Sam had died.

As if he'd read her thoughts, he asked abruptly, "How long ago did your husband die?"

"Three years."

"How?"

"He fell off the roof of this house." She wanted neither to talk about it nor think about it. Thinking about it might mean thinking about the reason she didn't want to live with Mark Logan, the reason she didn't want to live with any man.

One could avoid having one's husband ripped away—by not marrying at all.

Laguna Beach, California
Camille Logan's journal

Dear Diary,

I am so depressed. Alex Schoener is going out with Samantha Hetherington. Tish says it's just because Samantha has such big boobs, all the guys stare at her during P.E. whenever she runs, *and* she's a cheerleader. If only I could have made the squad. Tish says I had the highest score of all the girls who didn't make it, that I was just one point from Leigh MacDonald. Anyhow, I think Samantha's kind of fat. I can't wait to get my implants! Maybe then Alex will notice me.

And I sure don't want to go to Colorado this summer. If my dad wants to see me, why can't he come here? Then I can show off my implants on the beach. Tish got hers last year, and I could have, too, except I couldn't miss school. Mom would have let me, but if Dad ever found out...

He doesn't understand what it's like here, what's important. I'm going to ask Mom if I can ask a judge to let *me* decide whether or not I want to go to Colorado. Tish says I'm old enough, the court should listen to me, and I agree.

Samantha isn't that pretty. What does he like about her? She needs work done.

Chapter Two

Two weeks later

It was a Friday morning when Leah and Mary Grace climbed into their car and headed south toward the San Juan Mountains, the most rugged mountain range in Colorado. She had called Mark twice since his visit to her house, both times to make sure that she had packed the right clothing for herself and Mary Grace for their dog-sled trip. He'd been helpful, though brusque as ever. All her original dislike for him had been rekindled by his curt responses to her questions. The man was so rude she wondered how he managed to attract clients to his tours. But perhaps the clients thought his attitude was some proof of his competence in the backcountry. The more rude, the more self-sufficient, or something like that.

In any case, she had small hope of him showing sympathy for her current emotional upheaval. She'd prepared herself—tried to prepare herself—to relinquish this baby. The challenge of raising the child instead was blended with massive relief that she would not have to know the grief of her own loss that would have accompanied her sister's joy.

She was a little worried about leaving this weekend. One of her clients had experienced some spotting. The woman wasn't due for three months, and Leah's consulting physician had recommended a few days' bed rest. It was not a good time for Leah to be out of town. On the other hand, Leah had made an agreement with Mark Logan, and she felt she should keep her word.

And Corinne Cummings, the mother who was spotting, had been doing a lot. She was a professional athlete and slowing down wasn't usually part of her routine. She should be fine.

The weather was clear and the ground free of snow all the way into Montrose and most of the way to Ridgway. The distant mountains were snow-covered, of course, but not the ground near the highway. In Ridgway, they saw the first signs of snow, still collected in the fields along the road.

Leah pulled over briefly to consult the directions Mark had given her to the office of his business, Mount Sneffels Tours. Mount Sneffels was only one of the mountains in the San Juans, and Mark's tours ran throughout the region, but he said he'd always liked the name of the mountain, which had been christened after an Icelandic volcano.

The business office was all the way in the city of Ouray, ten miles south of Ridgway. Leah memorized the directions and started south again on the highway.

"Are we almost there?" Mary Grace asked. It was the first time she had asked this question. They had been listening to *The Hobbit* on tape the whole way so far.

"About fifteen minutes, I think," Leah answered.

"What will the dogs be like?" Mary Grace wanted a pet dog. Leah had agreed to a cat, but they hadn't selected one yet.

"I don't know. They are dogs whose job is to pull the sled."

"Are we both going to ride in the sled?"

"I don't know that either."

Leah turned off the tape because Mary Grace had embarked upon an inquisition, and she knew that she'd be answering questions all the way to Ouray.

So she tried to listen to her daughter, but what she was thinking of was the child she was carrying and the serious business of establishing a parenting relationship with Mark Logan.

MARK LEANED behind the counter of the cabin on Main Street which served as the office of Mount Sneffels Tours. He gazed out the window, watching for the blue Subaru which Leah Williams drove.

Mark still couldn't believe what River and Ellen had done. He had been willing to contribute his sperm to the baby project because River had asked him. And his brother's new lifestyle was one that Mark supported; he'd believed both he and Ellen would make good parents. So he'd said yes.

Now the original plan had fallen through. However,

if Ellen and River were not to raise his child, he would. He felt he'd been given a second chance at fatherhood. This time he'd do it right.

Leah Williams's being a midwife was excellent; she would have his baby by natural childbirth with no drugs clouding its entrance into life. He strongly believed that doing things the natural way was best. His business was dedicated to teaching people about nature so that their respect for it would increase, with a positive effect, he hoped, on how they conducted themselves in daily life. They would drive less, consume less, recycle what they could.

Sometimes Mark tried to remember when he'd had the first inklings that Sabrina had changed dramatically from the person she'd been when they'd married. Was it when she'd announced she was pregnant? *I'm taking advantage of every comfort medical science can offer,* his ex-wife had told him. *And, yes, I want tests. I want to know everything.*

He knew that it had been inappropriate for him to want to dictate the whys and wherefores of their child's birth. Granted, Sabrina's announcement that she would abort a child if she learned it was imperfect had repelled him—it still did. But what baffled him at the time was how much Sabrina seemed to have changed since their marriage. When they'd married, she'd said she loved his home up on Hastings Mesa, near the Dallas Divide, loved that it was off the grid, said she finally felt close to nature the way she'd always wanted to be. He'd believed they were compatible—and wanted the same things, the same kind of life together. But by the time she'd become pregnant with Camille, she'd begun trying to get him to buy a place in Telluride—as though they could afford it. She'd started spending all her free time up in Telluride, usually shopping. What she'd been shopping for, Mark had eventually learned, was husband number two. And what he now believed was that she'd been "trying on" the persona she'd shown early in their marriage; she'd liked the sound of it all, just not the reality.

The failure of their marriage wasn't all Sabrina's fault. He knew that. She'd complained that he was emotionally inaccessible and dictatorial. At some point, at least two years after marrying him, she'd said she wanted a man who didn't want to do everything "the hard way." He'd compromised. They'd acquired a washing machine, a coffeemaker, a CD player, a television and VCR, and a memory-foam mattress for their king-size bed.

But one day, Sabrina had announced that she hated having to start the generator on cloudy days, when there wasn't enough sunlight for the solar panels to power the electricity. She'd said that she no longer wanted to live off the grid. She'd said she wanted to live in the city.

But what she'd really wanted, he'd finally seen, was someone else. Someone he, Mark Logan, was not.

However, she'd also wanted his money, and she'd taken a lot of it when she'd left. The trade he'd made was to keep the business entirely his own.

Of course, Leah Williams showed no sign of being a gold digger—or the kind of woman who demanded weekly facials and pedicures—and she didn't seem particularly interested in him in any case. He imagined that she recycled without complaint. She probably preferred organic produce.

He bet she believed the world could be made a better place—and also felt sure that she would want to be part of that change.

Still, Mark didn't entirely know what to make of her. As far as he'd been able to figure out, she'd told him she was giving their child up for adoption simply to gauge his reaction.

It was unthinkable for him to give this child to just anyone. He hadn't expected to become a father again. He would be forty-seven on Monday. But now that he was responsible for the life of another child—well, he hoped to raise this baby as he'd not been able to raise Camille.

The Subaru pulled up outside, and he watched Leah get out. The back door opened, and a small girl with wheat-colored hair sprang out and stood beside her mother. No running into the street for this one. Her face, which showed the sharp and peculiarly elfin features of Leah, was sober and attentive to the world around her. She held a stuffed rabbit.

Mark watched them cross the street and went to the door to open it for them.

"Hi," Leah said. "I haven't brought in our stuff. I didn't know where you want me to leave the car."

"In the side lot." He tilted his head in the correct direction. "But you don't have to rush right out and move it. We'll drive to the trailhead in my vehicle. Nancy and Bob will meet us there with the dog sleds."

Leah looked down, then back to Mark's face. "Mark,

I think you've met my daughter, Mary Grace. Mary Grace, remember Mark? He's River's brother and he's the father of our baby."

Our baby. She meant, Mark realized, hers and Mary Grace's. Well, that perception would change if he had anything to say about it.

Mary Grace's eyes were her mother's, a brown so dark they were almost black. "Hello."

No shyness, hiding behind her mother, any of that. Mary Grace wore purple pants in a pile fabric and a purple snow jacket. Leah was dressed in tights, a long sweater and a navy-blue parka which curved gracefully over her rounded belly. Her long hair was bound in single loose braid.

Mark was struck again by just how beautiful she was. Her skin seemed poreless, and hers was the kind of beauty that couldn't be achieved with potions or surgery, only with healthful living.

He said, "Hello, Mary Grace. It's nice to meet you."

One of his employees, Darren, came in the back door. He would man the office this weekend. Mark made introductions, referring to Leah and Mary Grace as "friends" of his.

He offered them drinks from the cooler; Leah accepted pomegranate juice and Mary Grace a coconut protein smoothie, after convincing her mother that she would finish it.

Mark went out with them to help carry their bags— a large backpacking pack and one small day pack— from their car and to put them in his eight-year-old and very efficient dual-cab pickup truck with camper shell.

They settled in the vehicle, and Mark got behind the wheel and drove out onto the street, feeling happier than he had for a long time.

THE TRIP to the trailhead involved retracing the road Leah had driven from Ridgway, then driving up from Ridgway toward the Dallas Divide and the town of Telluride beyond. Mary Grace, in the backseat, sat solemnly looking out the window, sometimes forgetting to drink her smoothie, but not complaining that they were riding in a car again.

That was Mary Grace. Sam's death had cemented her personality. She seemed dedicated to being no trouble, a trait which sometimes concerned Leah. Children should be some trouble, but Mary Grace was almost too compliant.

Beside her, Mark drove with a casual confidence. His blond hair swept easily back from his face in loose curls over a very old gray sweatshirt with a blue-trimmed hood. He said, "I'd like you to see my house, too. It's off the road near Placerville."

"You drive all that way to Ouray to go to work?" Leah asked.

"Actually, there's an apartment above the office—I spend a lot of time there. I've installed some of the things I like to have at home, but I prefer the house."

"Things like?" Leah prompted.

"Solar panels, water-saving showerhead. I'm on a well at home."

"That's a nice way to live," Leah said, surprised by the wistful note in her own voice. "Sam and I planned on those kinds of conversions for our house, but—" She shrugged. *But then he died.* One minute he'd been there, her soul mate, the perfect spouse for her because their lives seemed so meant for each other. The next…

"You supervise home births?" he said.

The abrupt change in topic surprised Leah. "Yes," she said. "It's fairly safe where we are. There's a clinic close by with some emergency services, and the hospital is only fifteen minutes away. And our weather is not as variable as yours."

Indeed, the day which had begun so sunny had now clouded over as they drove higher up in the mountains.

"There's my house. You can just see it past those trees." He pointed out an A-frame structure beside the San Miguel River.

Leah glimpsed the solar panels winking under the clouds. "Did you build it?"

"I bought it half-completed. I finished it."

She gazed thoughtfully through the trees. "You were married."

"Yes."

"For how long?" Leah had a private belief that men over forty who'd never lived with someone or been married were very bad marital prospects. If a marriage was extremely short, it did not count, in her opinion.

"Well—four years on paper. Three in reality."

That was right at the edge of too short. "Lived with anyone else?" she asked and wondered why she was asking. It wasn't as though she was attracted to him. She just happened to be carrying a baby conceived with his sperm.

"Yes. Two years," he supplied before she could ask.

She felt as though they were circling each other, checking each other out, preparing to know each other better.

But I don't want a husband. I don't even want a boyfriend.

She'd made a business of protecting herself since Sam's death. Plenty of men were willing to prey on a newly widowed single mother—or so it had seemed to her. She seemed to attract men interested in the property she owned, interested in soothing her pain for their own ends, because she was vulnerable and they sensed it.

So Leah had made herself as invulnerable as possible, focusing on her work and on Mary Grace.

"How did you meet your husband?" Mark asked.

Leah smiled wistfully in recollection. "I was getting midwifery training at a school in Tennessee. It was on a sort of commune. He was just a regular guy—a carpenter in the nearby town. We met in the market. I was bringing eggs in from the farm where the school was. I slipped in some water on the floor, and he caught me and the eggs. It was rather beautiful."

Mark smiled. His teeth were even and white, his smile sexy.

"We were instantly attracted."

"You must miss him."

Leah turned to observe Mary Grace in the backseat, watching as her daughter fished in her own knapsack and brought out a Barbie doll. She did miss Sam. But she'd stopped thinking about it, had made herself move away from the grief. It was something that didn't benefit her, something she couldn't afford.

They came to a dirt road with a bridge leading across the river, up onto a forest-service road. Mark switched on his turn indicator and slowed. As he glanced behind him, he saw something which seemed to cause him irritation. He looked suddenly a bit grim.

"Everything all right?" Leah asked and looked behind her. The remains of Mary Grace's smoothie had spilled all over the backseat. "Mary Grace, that's why I said you needed to finish it." She started to unbuckle her seat belt, prepared to turn around and deal with the mess.

"We'll be there soon," Mark said. "Don't worry about it." He navigated the bridge carefully. The road was snow-packed.

Leah saw Mary Grace's lips begin to pout. Then she began to cry.

"Don't worry," Leah told her soothingly. "It's all right, and we're almost there."

But Mary Grace was still sobbing.

Then, they came upon the dog teams.

Two trucks were parked at the side of the road. Both held dog boxes, with individual places for perhaps a dozen dogs each.

Out in the snow, a woman and two men were harnessing teams of small husky-type dogs.

Mary Grace suddenly sat up as tall as she could in her seat, trying to peer out the front window. "Are we there?"

"Yes," Leah said.

Mary Grace unbuckled the restraint in her car seat and quickly figured out how to open the door for herself. Leah rummaged for one of the cloths she carried in her bag to clean up spills. She climbed out of the vehicle in time to see Mary Grace running toward the dogs and reaching out to pet one, startling the animal, which turned and snapped at her.

Mark was two steps behind Mary Grace and clasped her beneath the armpits, lifting her away from the dog team. Satisfied that he was dealing with that situation, Leah began cleaning the backseat, using water from one of her water bottles. A second later, Mary Grace was tugging at the hem of her coat, crying again. "It tried to bite me!"

The woman who had been harnessing dogs came over to the truck. She was almost six feet tall and very blond with a broad freckled face. "Hi, I'm Nancy." She crouched down beside Mary Grace. "Sweetie, it's a good idea to approach dogs slowly. And you should probably leave petting them for when Bob or I are with you."

Leah said, "I'm sorry she did that."

"It's fine. He didn't get you, did he?" Nancy asked Mary Grace.

"N-no," Mary Grace said, sniffing.

Leah felt eyes on her and turned to see Mark glance at them on the way to take their things from the truck. At the office in Ouray, he'd had them repack their belongings in special bags designed to be carried on the dog sleds. Now he said, "Everything okay?"

"Yes," Leah answered. But she wasn't sure that was

true. She should have been watching Mary Grace more closely. She was glad Mark had been.

MARK REMINDED himself that Mary Grace was only four, that she'd just been on a long car trip, that children spilled things and that they needed to be taught appropriate behavior around dogs. Well, he could help with the last. As the dogs strained at their harnesses, yipping and howling, eager to be off, he crouched down beside Mary Grace. "That was kind of scary, wasn't it?"

Mary Grace nodded solemnly. "They bite," she said with surprise.

"Pretty much everything with teeth can bite," Mark told her, "but they don't always. The thing is, these dogs are used to being with each other. And the way dogs sort each other out sometimes involves some nipping or clamping their jaws around each other's muzzles. It's how they work out who has the highest status."

Mary Grace frowned. "Do they hurt?"

Mark smiled. "No, they don't hurt each other. They nip and growl a bit to figure out who's the king and queen."

Mary Grace nodded thoughtfully.

"So now you know you're not supposed to approach the dogs or try to pet them unless you have Nancy or Bob or me with you."

"What about my mom?" Mary Grace asked as Leah approached them.

"The dogs don't know her yet. Now, you're going to ride in the sled," he said. "Do you want to get settled in?"

"I want to ride with my mom."

"She might be more comfortable standing on one of the runners."

"I'll ride in the sled with Mary Grace," Leah said, looking protective.

"Okay." He would drive the dog team, standing on the runners or running behind one sled. Nancy and Bob could put the luggage on the other sled.

He helped Leah and her daughter settle in the sled, with Mary Grace sitting in front. Suddenly the little girl laughed and turned around to look at her mother. "The baby jumped!"

"Yes," Leah replied, smiling.

Mark had a strange urge to put his hands on Leah's belly, so he could feel the baby's movements, too. He cleared his throat and asked gruffly, "Warm enough, you two?"

"Yes."

He consulted with Nancy and Bob. Then Mark stepped onto the runners of his sled, looking ahead to see the lead dog, a female named Jolly, looking back at him over the shoulder of her partner, Sid. He released the snow brake and called, "Hike!"

As THE cool air whipped around them, Leah put her face close to Mary Grace's and asked, "Do you like it?"

"Yes," said Mary Grace quietly.

"The dogs are happy," Leah told her. "I think they like to pull the sled. How many are there?"

Mary Grace sat up a little and counted. "Five…six… seven…eight!"

Leah hugged her daughter tightly and began to sing an old Donovan song. Then, from behind her, she heard the words sung in a rich baritone, blending with her soprano.

Awareness rippled over her. He liked to sing, too. Now that she was spending time with him, she was softening her attitude toward him. Maybe they could make their arrangement work after all.

They stopped once for a snack and to let the dogs rest, and Leah said she'd like to stand on one of the runners for a while when they started again.

"Will you be able to balance?" Mark asked. "I don't want you to fall."

"I'll be fine."

Nancy asked Leah, "When is your baby due?"

"July thirty-first."

"We have two at home," Nancy said. "My sister's watching them. They're six and ten."

"Do they ever come and help on trips?"

"Sometimes. It's hard for them, because they know they have to work, they can't complain. They have to be older than they are, if you know what I mean."

"I do," Leah replied, liking the other woman.

She was glad for the baby inside her, keeping her warm in the brisk March air. "Mary Grace, will you be okay sitting in the sled alone so I can stand up for a while?"

"Yes," Mary Grace said.

With her fur-trimmed hood around her face, she looked like a small princess. Leah's heart swelled with love for her. She turned to Mark and said, "Thank you for doing this for us."

"You're welcome."

He looked even more handsome under the spring sky, outdoors, clearly in his element. He was the quintessential mountain man, Ellen had always said, and Leah could see that in him now. It troubled her that she was noticing his looks so much, that she was finding herself…well, she couldn't be attracted to him.

It was all hormones, all simple physical desire. And not so strong, Leah told herself, that she couldn't ignore it.

They set off again, and this time Leah stood on one of the sled's runners while Mark stood on the other. He was very tall, she thought. He seemed ready to catch her if she should lose her balance, though Leah had no idea how he would manage that.

As a turn approached, he said, "Lean a bit inside now. Not too far."

She stayed on, but she found it wasn't as easy as he had made it look.

Before dark they reached the hut where they would spend the night. Nancy, Bob and Mark carried sleeping bags, mats and camping gear inside. Mary Grace had fallen asleep on the sled, and she awoke when they reached the hut. She clung to Leah's parka with one small, mittened hand.

There were bunk beds inside, and Mark laid out Leah's sleeping bag on the lower bunk of one, on the thin firm mattress. The hut was equipped with a woodstove and firewood, and soon a blaze was going, heating the small cabin. Nancy and Bob did the cooking on small camp stoves, and Leah's offers of help were politely refused.

"You relax," Nancy said. "You're pregnant, and you put in a long day."

It had been an easy day as far as Leah was concerned, but she gladly relaxed in front of the woodstove with Mary Grace, who had taken out her Barbie dolls again.

Nancy said, "Mary Grace, tell me about your dolls." She crouched down on the floor beside the four-year-old.

"This is Keira," Mary Grace began, "and this is Agnes. Agnes looks like my mom."

"Yes, I see the resemblance. They're both very pretty."

"Keira has a pet monster. He lives in a cave near the river at our house."

The river Mary Grace meant was the irrigation ditch, where she sometimes sailed boats made of sticks and leaves.

"He's green," Mary Grace said, "and his tail is thirty-five feet long."

Nancy asked, "What does he eat?"

"Bugs."

Mark stared thoughtfully at Mary Grace and her dolls. "Camille used to love Barbies."

His daughter, Leah thought. The sixteen-year-old in Laguna Beach. She wanted to learn more about Camille, but she didn't want to do so in front of Nancy and Bob.

They ate dinner around the woodstove, and afterward Leah insisted on helping scrub the pots outside in the snow. Mark joined her.

Leah asked, "Does Camille come on trips like this with you when she visits?"

"She has done. It's a little harder to get her out in the wilderness now that she's older, but once we're out here together she seems to have a good time." Mark lifted his blue eyes to glance at Leah as he washed a pot with biodegradable soap and water collected from melted snow.

"She's lucky you spend time with her," Leah said. "Plenty of noncustodial fathers never bother."

"I'd have her all the time if it was up to me," he admitted. "But it's not. And her mom doesn't encourage it. In fact, I'd say she sometimes makes things pretty difficult. And Camille seems to have picked up her values."

"Such as?"

He raised one hand and touched the bump on his nose. "She didn't like the Logan nose she inherited, so she had a nose job."

"Didn't you have to give your approval?" Leah asked, squatting across from him on the snow. She spent a lot of time squatting while pregnant because she knew it would help her in labor.

He shook his head. "I let her have full custody in return for my eight weeks a year visitation—which the judge considered generous. Now Camille wants breast augmentation."

Leah closed her eyes for a moment. She had known women so unhappy with their appearance that they'd wanted to change things about themselves. Granted, few of them chose plastic surgery. It wasn't common in Paonia. But at sixteen…

"Camille's a pretty girl. She was pretty before she had all these things done. And each thing she does seems like a choice to make herself less unique."

Impulsively—and naturally—Leah reached across and put her hand on his arm.

He said, "You should get back inside and stay warm."

She dropped her hand and shrugged.

"Your daughter has a good imagination," he told her. "I like her."

"She's very self-possessed," Leah answered.

"I've been accused," he said, "of being rigid."

"No," Leah said in mock surprise.

He laughed.

She liked him then, liked him for his ability to laugh at himself.

And that fact troubled her. She didn't want to like him, to be attracted to him. She did not want to be married or even involved; to be either was to risk being left alone.

Mary Grace appeared in the doorway. "Mommy, where are you? I want you to come inside."

Leah stood up at once, answering her daughter's call.

MARY GRACE began whining first thing the next morning. She didn't want to wear her clean sweater, saying she hated it. She did not like her oatmeal. She was cold and wanted to go home.

"We're on our way home," Leah assured her as she bundled Mary Grace into her seat on the sled and settled behind her to hug her tightly, hoping to cheer her out of her mood.

"Will we be there soon?" Mary Grace asked.

"Tonight you can sleep in your own bed," Leah answered.

Mark did not seem impatient with Mary Grace's bad temper. At one point, he used the brake to halt the sled and dogs, and crouched beside Mary Grace and Leah. He smiled at the four-year-old. "You know what? You're really a trouper. It really helps when people don't complain, because when you're out in the wilderness it's not easy for anyone. We encourage each other, and that makes things easier."

What a wonderful thing to tell her, Leah thought. He was being a wise coach, and she saw Mary Grace swell with pride at his praise. Also, she whined less afterward.

The hours flew till they reached the parking area. Two minutes after they started for Ouray with Mark driving, Mary Grace was asleep.

Leah said, "She was good."

"I agree," Mark said.

"She isn't always," Leah admitted.

"I noticed."

Leah glanced at him, but he was smiling. She tried to remember an incident when Mary Grace *hadn't* been good. Well, she'd spilled her drink. And she'd whined a bit. But she couldn't imagine any four-year-old behaving any better than her daughter had. Could Mark Logan? She said, "You've had better-behaved children on trips with you?"

"Better and worse," he said.

"A better-behaved four-year-old," she said, unable to keep a challenging note out of her voice.

"Actually, at that age, Camille was amazing. She still is," he said, sounding wistful.

All Leah's warm feelings toward Mark evaporated.

She didn't like that he compared Mary Grace to Camille. She prayed he wouldn't do the same when their child was born. She didn't want Mary Grace to grow up in an environment where anyone counted her as second best.

Laguna Beach, California
Camille's journal

Dear Diary,

There's a new guy at school, and he's *sooo* cute. This is his first time going to a public school. He's always gone to Waldorf Schools, and he plays the piano really well, Tish says. He's going to school at LBH because it's closer to his new teacher. He used to live in New Mexico, and his name is James Salazar. He looks kind of Latino but kind of Indian, too. He's also supposed to be a really good basketball player. It's like I totally don't care about Alex now. I saw James looking at me during Trig today. I hardly want to eat.

Chapter Three

Their trip had been what he'd promised, a chance for him to get to know Leah and Mary Grace—and the reverse. Leah had learned that his birthday was the Monday after they returned from the trip. She and Mary Grace made him a card which she knew would arrive a day late. She also left him a message on his cell phone thanking him for the trip and wishing him a happy birthday. He called back while she was seeing a client and left a message saying he'd enjoyed the trip, too.

All in all, Leah was satisfied that she and Mark could become good friends in the long run. And that could only make sharing parenting responsibilities that much easier.

He seemed determined to keep in touch with her as her pregnancy progressed. He called every few days and came to Paonia two weeks after their dog-sled trip. He picked up Leah and Mary Grace and took them to the dinosaur museum in Fruita, a little over an hour away, then to lunch at a Thai restaurant in Grand Junction.

He asked to come to a prenatal appointment with

Leah's midwife, who lived in Delta, between Paonia and Mark's home in the San Juan Mountains. Leah agreed to this and chose an appointment which fell during her twenty-seventh week of pregnancy, on May Day.

She had prepared the midwife, Kassandra, for this when she called her the week after the dog-sled trip to shuffle the appointment so that it would work with Mark's schedule.

Kassandra was twenty-seven and had never given birth herself. She and Leah had covered clients for each other in the past, and Leah liked the other woman. Kassandra had overseen the artificial insemination.

"There's been a change," Leah had said when she reached Kassandra on the phone. She'd pictured the dark-haired woman with her elegant little horn-rimmed glasses, eyes sharpening behind them.

"A change?"

"Ellen is pregnant."

"Ellen?"

"My sister, Ellen. The mother-to-be—well, we thought—of this child."

"Right." Pause. "She's pregnant." Disbelief modulated by professionalism. "And that changes things?"

"Yes. I'm going to keep the baby, and Mark Logan, whom you met, is going to fulfill his role as father. So he'll be coming with me to the next appointment."

Kassandra let out a breath. "How do you feel about all of this, Leah? I know that you've said you didn't want to raise another child."

"Well. I've adjusted. Or, I'm adjusting. Or something like that. But I want the baby. Now that Ellen's—done this—"

"How did Ellen do that? Not that it matters, but…"

"She'd thought they couldn't conceive together. It wasn't anyone's fault."

"Well, my concern is you and your baby. Do you want to meet before our next appointment, without the father there?"

"No need," Leah said. "As I said, I've— Well, actually, once I got over the shock— It will be fine," she concluded lamely. Granted, she and Mark Logan were neither partners nor lovers. They would each be single parents. Leah wasn't sure she wanted a partner or lover, even if Mark *was* interested.

That was the kind of thing Kassandra was willing to talk about.

But Leah couldn't talk. She couldn't imagine making this very nice, sober and responsible young woman understand what it was to bear a child, to begin to raise a child, with one's lover and husband and fellow dream-builder, only to lose that partner.

Now she was alone, and since carrying this new child, even more alone. More alone in responsibility. More alone with what she bore—and with whom, the new person who would call her mother.

Kassandra seemed to read that it wasn't as simple as Leah was making out, but she didn't press her client. She said, "Then, I'll see you both in a few weeks. But, Leah, please call any time. What you're going through isn't easy. I'm your midwife—and your friend, don't forget."

"Thank you," Leah said.

IT WAS a morning appointment. When Leah arrived home from taking Mary Grace to her Montessori preschool, she found Mark's truck, this time without camper shell, in her driveway. He was walking around the exterior of her small one-story ranch house, inspecting the siding and eaves, but looked up at the approach of her Subaru.

He smiled, and her heart thudded strangely.

This isn't good, Leah told herself.

It wasn't good that she'd dressed carefully for the morning either, in a black maternity dress that was a cast-off from a woman whose birth she'd attended the previous spring. The dress made her look slender, fertile, pregnant, old-fashioned. Or so she believed. She'd braided her hair in one long herringbone braid which hung down her back, and she wore some onyx earrings with cameos which Ellen had made for her.

Mark walked toward her from the side of the house.

"Did it pass your inspection?" Leah asked.

"Looks like it's painting time."

No doubt, but her budget couldn't stretch to hiring painters just now, and she was reluctant to expose herself to the fumes. She gave the latter excuse.

He said, "I think you'll be okay. It's the exterior, after all."

And it wasn't early in her pregnancy, when the baby would have been most susceptible to teratogenic influences. But Leah didn't care to let him in on her financial circumstances and so made no reply.

"Would you let me do that for you?" he asked.

"Paint the house?"

"Sure. I'll even buy the paint."

The question wasn't simple. Paint for her house would not be inexpensive. She had no doubt that he could do a good job; she was certain he'd never have offered if that wasn't the case. But if she accepted she would be indebted to him. "I wouldn't let you buy the paint," she said at once.

But accept his labor?

Strange. Part of her midwifery care involved educating fathers on how they could help pregnant moms— and also, in certain instances, stressing to mothers that they *should* accept help, accept it as a nurturing of the child by the father.

So why did she find her own advice so hard to follow?

He seemed to read her mind. "It doesn't need to mean anything, Leah. Accept that I care about you and our baby, and I want to make your lot easier."

She forced herself to hear her own advice and to heed it. "Okay. Thank you, then."

"Have you tried underground drip irrigation, by the way?"

"We meant to, when Sam was alive. But he died before it happened. River works the orchard now, and it would be inappropriate for him to install a new system seeing as it's not his land."

"I could do it."

"Materials aren't cheap," she said.

"They don't have to be expensive either. Let me work it up for you. It would increase your property value some and help you do things more efficiently if you ever wanted to care for the orchard yourself."

She hesitated.

He smiled, and the smile seemed like that of an older brother—amused, protective, respectful, all at once. "You're a fairly independent woman, aren't you?"

Leah shrugged. "I guess I am." She changed the subject to take the focus off herself—and off the ways he was proposing to help her. "Shall we head to Delta? Do you want to use the bathroom or get something to drink first?"

"I'm fine."

They took her car, but she allowed Mark to drive and was grateful not to have to.

"Who are we going to see?" he asked on the way.

"Kassandra. You met her when…" Her voice trailed off. Good grief, Leah. You're a midwife, she thought. You talk about these things every day.

His eyes flicked from the road for one instant, to take in her flush, she was sure.

"Yes, when," he agreed with a teasing grin.

KASSANDRA'S office was in a yellow house on a side street in Delta. She shared a waiting room with a marriage and family therapist and with an acupuncturist in a business that fell under the curtain name of West Delta Health Services. No one else was waiting, and when they arrived Kassandra showed them into her examining room at once. The walls were pale yellow and covered with photos of children Kassandra had helped birth—there were about seventy-five of these—and charts showing the fetus at different stages of development. The latter reminded Leah to change the chart on her own refrigerator. She kept one there so that Mary Grace could see at what stage her sister or brother was in growth.

Kassandra said, "It's nice to see you," to Mark, and she and Leah began the usual prenatal checks. Blood pressure, urine tests, weight gain.

Then Leah climbed up on the table so that Kassandra could measure her abdomen and check the baby's lie. Kassandra gave her a clean flannel sheet to put over the lower half of her body so that she could simply pull up her dress to reveal her abdomen.

Mark said, "Do you want me to go out?"

Kassandra looked at Leah.

"You can stay," Leah said. He wanted to be this baby's father in practice as well as in fact. His being in on this part of the prenatal care seemed like a good idea. In truth, she found herself grateful that he cared.

Putting her measuring tape against Leah's smooth, rounded abdomen, Kassandra said to Mark, "I'm measuring from the top of the pubic bone to the fundus or top of the uterus. At this stage, the baby should be growing about one centimeter a week. We are at twenty-seven centimeters, exactly right on for Leah's due date."

She took out a fetoscope and warmed it with her hand. "I'm going to listen for the baby's heart tones now, and you can listen, too," she told Mark. "They sound a bit muffled and distant and faster than an adult's." She moved the fetoscope around on Leah's belly, listening until she found the baby's heartbeat. She measured the heart rate, then pulled the earpieces from her ears and offered them to Mark.

He bent over, thinking his own heartbeat might somehow be known to everyone in the room. Leah's skin was smooth and soft. She had a small tattoo of a hummingbird on the left side of her rib cage, beneath her breast. The image suited her, he thought. She was joyful yet fierce. And she seemed tireless— or that had been his experience of her during the dog-sled trip.

He listened through the fetoscope, listened past other sounds until he heard it. The quiet beat that made him think, perhaps because of Leah's tattoo, of hummingbird wings. He carefully drew back.

He watched Kassandra check Leah's belly with her hands and wished that he had a camera with him to record the midwife's slender hands against Leah's smoothly rounded belly. The experience sent an eerie hush over him, a holy quiet. Kassandra explained that she was checking the baby's presentation.

Meeting Leah's eyes, Kassandra said, "Transverse."

"Oh, great," Leah said.

But she and Kassandra both knew ways to attempt to turn the baby. Leah wasn't sure she felt like trying any of those things in front of Mark Logan, but then she thought, Why not?

Kassandra said, "Let's do your internal exam, and then we'll try turning her."

Kassandra, Leah knew, frequently referred to

babies in utero as her. Leah alternated between her and him, trying to do so equally in the case of unknown sex.

Mark, who had been quiet since he'd heard the baby's heart, said, "I can step out."

"You don't have to," Leah said. She met Kassandra's eyes and saw the midwife's small expression of surprise. They both knew that the chance of turning the baby was greatest if Leah was most relaxed.

Mark sat down and moved his chair over near her head.

Leah shifted to make her hair more comfortable around the back of her braid, and he moved the pillow beneath her head.

Her heart raced. She listened as Kassandra reported the findings of the internal exam, all good. Kassandra disposed of her rubber gloves and said, "What do you think, Leah?"

"Hands and knees," Leah decided.

She sat up, and Kassandra held the flannel sheet around her as she turned onto her hands and knees on the table.

"Your job," Kassandra said to Mark, "is to help her relax."

"Then maybe I should leave," he said.

Leah burst out laughing and felt her face flush so that she scarcely noticed Kassandra's hands on her abdomen. "What's that supposed to mean?"

"That I don't think my presence—in general—has a relaxing effect on you."

He was sitting, and she could look into his face,

which seemed very near. "Just as long as you don't turn off the electricity in my house."

It was a weak and silly joke, but Mark surprised her by laughing. "No, but I might take away your washing machine."

She appreciated the joke, his being willing to poke fun at his own sometimes extreme beliefs.

"And make me sew my own clothes."

"And mine," he told her.

Kassandra listened to the baby's heart, then let the fetoscope slide down around her neck. "Did it," Kassandra said with satisfaction. "I think you should bring him next time, too."

Leah sat and let her dress fall down.

Mark's hand helped her rearrange the dress, and Leah found herself trembling.

I like him touching me.

Damn.

THEY WALKED out of the clinic together, and Mark said, "Feel like breakfast? Maybe an early lunch?"

"Sure. I am hungry. But let's try The Soup, in Paonia."

"Great."

Twenty minutes later, they sat at a booth in one of Paonia's two vegetarian restaurants, beside a billboard advertising massage services, the farmers' market, crystal readings, astrological counseling and a new indie film at the small local theater. Leah ordered an omelet and Mark huevos rancheros.

She said, "Thank you for coming to the appointment

with me. You really did keep my mind off what she was doing. Or rather—kept it from filling with transverse-lie nightmares."

"Explain what that means."

"It means that neither the head nor the butt was presenting. If the baby is in transverse lie when I go into labor and can't be turned, he has to be born by cesarean section."

"That could make you nervous," he agreed. "Is the baby likely to turn back?"

"I'm not going to think about it," she told him. "I keep my thoughts as positive as possible during pregnancy."

Mark found he couldn't take his eyes from her face. His heart had swelled, and he understood what all the emotions rushing through him meant. This woman was perfect for him. She matched some inner picture inside him of what the mother of his child—and, more uneasily, what his partner in life—should be. She was so different from Sabrina. "I think I'm falling in love with you," he said.

She flushed, the color doubling on her high cheekbones. "I think that's because I'm carrying your child."

She kept her eyes lowered, and he didn't argue with her because he hadn't intended to say that in the first place.

He said, "You remind me of a Celtic goddess, one of those women you see in pictures, riding chariots drawn by oversize dogs."

"Stop it," she said firmly, grabbing the orange juice the waitress had brought and spilling part of it, first on the tablecloth, then down her chin.

He laughed and reached across with the napkin, his hand lingering against her jaw as he briefly dabbed at her chin. He let go and stared at his hand as if it had betrayed him.

Just then, the door of the café opened, and a woman strode in, one of Ellen's friends. Leah knew her slightly. Danine Luce was tall, in her early forties, with a long blond braid and a beautiful smile. Danine was a life coach and author of self-help books. She was a vegan and made most of her money through direct marketing companies that sold expensive health products. She had been a model and an actress before she came to Paonia, on the rebound after a breakup with a success-ful financier. She had two children, one of them a girl Mary Grace's age.

Leah did not particularly like her.

Mark looked up. "Danine," he said in surprise.

"Well, look who came down from the mountains," Danine responded in a rich, low voice, ignoring Leah.

Mark stood to greet her, and the blonde gave him a quick hug. "How's the season been?"

"Excellent, for as little snow as we've had. Leah, have you met Danine?"

"Yes," Leah said. "Mary Grace goes to preschool with Danine's daughter, Astra."

"And, of course, we've talked about midwifery," said Danine. "Because that's part of my background, too."

It was part of her background in that Danine had given birth to Astra without an attendant. She consid-ered herself a "spiritual midwife" because of this. She had also provided emotional support to a friend in labor. Kassandra had attended the birth and been reticent about Danine; Leah had realized that Kassandra did not care for the woman either.

"Look, I've got to run. I just came in for a shot of wheatgrass juice. Then I have a conference call with a client from Denver. Mark, get in touch. I'd be glad to give you some feedback on your business goals."

"Thank you," he said, though Leah was pleased to see that he looked taken aback at the suggestion that he would need Danine's help achieving—or even defining—his business goals.

While Danine headed for the counter, Mark sat down again.

"Old friend?" Leah asked.

He shrugged.

Leah wondered if he was attracted to Danine. Had they dated? Surely he could see through her pretense.

He changed the subject. "So, do you want to go with the same colors on your house?"

Leah felt a buzzing vibration against her leg. Her cell phone.

She withdrew it from her pocket to check if it was a client's number.

It was Ellen's.

Well, Ellen was a client.

Leah pushed back from the table and stood up. "Excuse me, Mark, I have to get this." She answered the phone as she walked toward the restaurant's glass door and stepped outside.

"Leah. Thank God. Leah, I'm spotting. And I have cramps."

Ellen was in her thirteenth week of pregnancy. Spotting and cramps at this stage were not a good sign. They pointed—dramatically, it seemed to Leah, seemed to her now—to imminent miscarriage.

And what would Ellen expect then? That Leah should give up the child she had come to think of as hers?

But Ellen's voice was teary.

Leah said, "Okay, relax, first thing. If you do miscarry, and that's by no means certain, it will probably be because the baby wasn't viable, all right? It's sort of a divine prenatal test. So just relax now and tell me when this started. Tell me everything."

She listened as Ellen described the cramps that had begun an hour before and the bloody show she'd subsequently found on her underwear.

"What were you doing?" Leah asked.

"I was pulling weeds in the border outside the house, around the mints."

"Which mints?" But Leah knew and cursed her own inattention to this detail of her sister's pregnancy. How was Ellen supposed to know?

"The lemon and the pennyroyal."

"All right. Keep away from the pennyroyal. That's probably what did it. Wash your hands very thoroughly to get any of the oil off and go lie down. I'm having breakfast with Mark, and I'll have him bring me right over afterward. I'm going to give you a recipe for a brew that River can prepare for you. Is he there?"

"No. He's over at your place in the orchard."

"Then, go do what I told you and don't worry. I'll be over right away."

Leah gave herself another kick for not telling her sister about pennyroyal, which Leah had known grew outside her sister's kitchen window and which was a natural abortifacient. Ellen should have no contact with the oil in pregnancy. If Leah hadn't been busy subconsciously resenting her sister's entirely unforeseeable pregnancy she would have thought to warn Ellen about the pennyroyal.

I have to focus on her now.

Not only did she want Ellen's pregnancy to go well for her sister's sake, now Leah felt an urgency of her own connected with that baby. If Ellen miscarried...

But Leah wasn't going to think about that.

She closed her phone and hurried back into the restaurant to tell Mark that they would have to take their meal to go.

Laguna Beach, California
Camille's journal

Dear Diary,

James talked to me today! I couldn't believe it. It was during break, and I was in the library looking for Tish, and he saw me and started talking to me. He said I seem smart—because I'm good at Trig. He's so easy to talk to! I'm so glad I wore my Jimmy Choos today.

We're both on yearbook, too, though it's so late in the year almost everything has been done. We talked about Jessica Bates, because she's Prettiest this year, and she's also one half of Cutest Couple.

James said something totally weird. He said Jessica looks like everybody else, and then he also said her body reminds him of a cartoon character because she's skinny like me but has huge tits. I said that it's what looks good, and he just shrugged.

It bugs me that he is definitely going to notice my implants when I get them. Of course, most guys just want you to have them. Like Colin— he just said once, "If you don't like your body, you can fix it, can't you?" That's definitely my philosophy. There are so many beautiful girls and not enough cute guys to go around. You've got to do every little thing you have to get an edge.

I'm starting jogging every day and going to aerobics class with Tish. But it'll be a while before I'm thin enough and until I get my implants to show off my body on the beach! Ugh. Some days I hate myself.

Chapter Four

Pulling up outside Ellen and River's house, an "Earthship" model built into one of the rolling hills of their property, Mark asked, "Shall I come in with you?"

"Yes, actually. I might be able to use your help." Though the infusion she planned to prepare for Ellen was a simple affair and Leah had the herbs in her midwifery bag, the bag she'd taken with her to her appointment, if any of the ingredients were missing she might have to send Mark out for them.

Strange that she suddenly felt she could count on him for something like that. But who had ever suggested he wasn't dependable? He had a reputation as a man who could keep you alive in the wilderness, a man who didn't do abandonment.

Maybe Ellen and River hadn't chosen so badly when they'd selected River's brother for their child's father.

As Leah climbed out of his car, she hoisted her midwifery bag to her shoulder. She had pared down its contents, had divided her birth kit between two bags so as not to be constantly lifting something so heavy.

Leah knocked on the front door with its knocker which declared Not All Who Wander Are Lost.

Ellen's voice called from inside. "Come in!"

Leah opened the door and stepped inside with Mark. She removed her shoes, and so did he—more of an effort in his case as he wore work boots.

A cell phone rang, and Leah realized it was his.

"Sorry," he said, preparing to answer.

Leah went ahead into River and Ellen's bedroom. Her sister was on the water bed, looking pale and anxious.

"I don't want to lose the baby, Leah," were the first words from her sister's mouth.

"There's no reason to think that's going to happen. Let's give you a quick check—I won't do an exam, because we don't want to disturb things unnecessarily. Then, I'm going to make you an infusion and leave instructions for how much and how often to take it."

When Leah went out to the kitchen a few minutes later, Mark was still on his cell phone. She began heating water on the stove for the herbal infusion, finding a jar in which to brew the remedy, as Mark said, "I don't agree with that, Sabrina. I didn't agree with the nose job. Anyhow, you can't take her out of school for that, or you will be hearing from my attorney. And her visitation has been set up six months in advance. You've received notice of it by certified mail. So she is coming to Colorado at the planned time."

Curious and unable to keep from overhearing, she carefully measured cramp bark and raspberry leaves into a reusable muslin tea bag and set the tinctures she would add to the infusion on the counter.

"Yes, Tish can come with her," Mark said. "I have no problem with one of Camille's friends staying with her here in Colorado." A pause. "That may be true, Sabrina, but that isn't going to change the visitation dates…. Yes, well, you put that before a judge. I doubt that even in California judges will change a teenager's visitation date so that she can have breast augmentation surgery."

Oh, thought Leah. *Poor Mark.* Without hearing the other side of the conversation, she could imagine the impact this dispute would have on his summer visitation with his daughter. Camille would resent his refusal to let her have the cosmetic surgery, resent his refusal to change his visitation time so that it could be scheduled. And if Mark's ex-wife had full custody, well, that was the only way he could even postpone the procedure.

Leah didn't bring up the subject until they were headed back to her house from Ellen's, leaving her sister resting. Ellen was no longer cramping; the crisis may have passed.

She asked Mark about the phone call carefully. "You were talking to your ex-wife?"

"About Camille's summer visit," he acknowledged.

Leah glanced at him questioningly.

"I'm sure you overheard enough. Camille wants breast-enlargement surgery."

Leah gave a small smile. "I think they like to call it 'enhancement.'"

"Who would 'they' be?"

She shrugged. "The industry."

"You know something about it?"

She nodded. "Actually, yes. One of my clients was a plastic surgeon—not a cosmetic surgeon. We became good friends."

"I'm surprised she discussed the issue with you."

"Well, she's an interesting woman. She worked at a military hospital. Did her residency there, that is. She specialized in reconstructive surgery, and it offended her somewhat that cosmetic surgeons—those she perceived as focusing exclusively on cosmetic surgery—stigmatized plastic surgery, which is a necessary medical specialty."

"Ah."

"But she said a number of things I hadn't thought about. Women aren't simply getting face lifts and breast implants, they're getting work on virtually every part of their bodies. Feet? Can you imagine?"

She saw the look of horror crossing his face.

"But the bottom line, this client of mine pointed out, was that whatever cosmetic surgery achieves—cosmetic as opposed to reconstructive—the problem is the pressure women feel to look a certain way. That how they look is who they are." Leah paused. "Sorry. I didn't mean to go on and on about this."

Mark smiled grimly. "That's exactly what I'm afraid of for Camille. She shouldn't feel she has to have surgery to be valuable, to have personal worth. God, she's beautiful already, but that's not what gives her value as a person."

Leah was silent, but only for a moment. "Just out of curiosity, have you told your daughter or her mother about this baby?"

The silence lingered, and so she looked over at him.

"No. I've been thinking about it. To be perfectly honest, what happened doesn't show me in the most responsible light."

"Because you were a sperm donor?"

"And because it has all turned out…differently than I expected."

Leah couldn't suppress a small sigh.

"I'm happy about the outcome, Leah, excited about this child. It's just that my life's work involves foreseeing the future, looking out for hazards, making the right choice. This time I left a lot to chance."

Leah understood his feelings. Her own were similar. They both had acted a bit rashly, conceiving a child to give to Ellen and River. It was certainly unconventional. Mary Grace, age four and completely remarkable, had accepted the whole situation as a fascinating novelty. But how would a sixteen-year-old daughter and an ex-wife react?

"I have a question for you," Mark said.

"Yes."

"Ellen seems to be in danger of miscarrying."

"That's always a possibility." Her voice squeaked, too high, embarrassing. Good grief. His was a reasonable question.

"What will you do if she does?"

Leah swallowed. Now, her voice shook. "I've decided to keep this child, Mark."

He continued looking forward, and she saw him nod.

"I never planned to do it with you," she said.

He didn't answer.

DRIVING BACK to Ouray, Mark turned over all the logistical problems of Leah's pregnancy. He was not going to let go of this child the way he had Camille. He and Sabrina had divorced when Camille was three, and he'd tried his best to be a good father, calling Camille weekly and taking every visitation. But he hadn't been able to control the fact that Camille was becoming less and less what he'd wanted her to be.

He'd wanted her to grow up much as he and River had. Their parents had been hippies living on a small farm in Utah. He'd chosen life in the mountains rather than farming, but he'd hoped Camille could grow up off the grid, living simply, developing wholesome values. Instead, she cared about *stuff*. And wanted cosmetic surgery.

Sabrina had called him an "organic fascist" and accused him of needing to control everything. There was enough truth in both accusations to make him wonder how much of their problems had been his doing. Why couldn't he find a woman who liked a simple life? That was the question he'd asked himself for years.

But he seemed to have found one. The only problem was, Leah was rooted in her life in Paonia. His livelihood lay in the mountains. There were no outfitters down where Leah lived, except river outfitters who ran white-water raft trips. Mark could run a river outfit; he had the experience, had worked as a river guide, had outfitted mountain trips. But permits, permits to guide river trips on the Gunnison River, were unavailable. He'd have to buy permits from another outfitter, and he knew the price would stretch him, even if someone was selling.

Would Leah be willing to relocate her practice to the mountains?

But he thought of his home, realized how inaccessible it was in the winter, how difficult it would be for her to get in and out to attend births. People counted on her. Also, because of the weather in the mountains, most women chose to birth in the hospital in Montrose, knowing they couldn't reach help quickly if there was a problem with a home birth.

No. He had to find a way to move to Paonia. And to show Leah that she needed him there.

MARK'S weekly conversations with his daughter had gotten shorter and shorter over the past four or five years. He'd spent two hours with an adolescent counselor to learn how best to speak to his daughter during these conversations, how to draw her out. Through this, he'd learned how to get her to talk, but he hadn't yet figured out how to hide his own feelings about some of the things she had to say. That Sunday night's conversation began typically—typically, except that he was listening less attentively than usual, nervous about what he had to impart.

I'm going to be a father again. You're going to have a half brother or sister.

But it was hard even to be properly preoccupied as he read the undercurrents of the connection.

Camille was very cool and seemed to have nothing to say.

Not a word.

"What did you do this week?" he asked.

"The usual."

"Being?"

"Went to school, went to aerobics, hung out with friends, did my homework. Can I go now?"

"We just started talking."

"I don't really feel like it."

Manipulation. Mark recognized the technique. His daughter was going to try to punish him for standing in the way of her getting breast-augmentation surgery, or whatever it was called.

"Why not?" he asked.

"I just don't."

"You're mad that I'm insisting on going ahead with our visitation plan," he guessed, knowing he was right.

"Whatever."

She was good at this, Mark reflected. "You're not going to change my mind on this, Camille. Why do you want to change yourself, anyhow?" He felt strange asking. He really didn't want to talk to his daughter about her breasts, didn't think he should have to, felt incapable of doing so effectively, and knew that within seconds he'd be resorting to clichés like, *You're perfect as God made you.* And, *Why would you want to be inauthentic?*

"We don't have to talk about it," she said coldly. "You couldn't possibly understand."

She was right about that, Mark decided immediately. But he wanted to understand—sort of. Mostly he wanted the bizarre situation to resolve itself, to go away.

"Camille," he said, "if you ever want to see a counselor, talk to someone about…things…you know I'll pay."

"I don't need to talk to anyone. I know what I want, and it's no different from what other girls my age want."

Mark wondered if this was true. Would Leah know? Their conversations hadn't ventured into the realm of the average teenage girl. He had a feeling Leah Williams had never been average in her life.

Of course, neither was Camille.

But isn't that what bothers you, Mark? That she wants to be just like her peers?

And he considered her peers shallow, corrupted by television and commercialism, branded by corporations whose logos those teenagers had been taught to want to display.

Kids in Colorado weren't like that; at least, he didn't think so. He didn't know any Colorado kids who'd had plastic surgery or who got new highlights and Brazilian bikini waxes every three weeks.

"Look, Dad, Colorado's boring for me. I don't want to go there for eight weeks. It's almost the whole summer. I want to go to the beach and be with my friends here."

Was that true? No, he decided. It was a lie. "What you want," he said, "is cosmetic surgery, and I'm completely against it."

"You know, Tish says I'm old enough that a judge will let me choose if I don't want visitation."

"I think the judge might take a dim view of your reasons for not wanting it."

"I'm sixteen. And I don't want to go to Colorado. Why do you want me to come there when I don't want to go?"

His throat swelled. He tried to speak, tried to say, *Because you're my daughter, and I want to know you.* Or, *Because I love you.*

He said instead, "It's good for you."

"It is not. It's not good for anyone to do things they don't want to do."

"Wrong. Which is why it's important for you to come to Colorado. In California, you make the rules. When you live with me, I do."

"It's just about proving you really have some impact on my life?"

Mark felt everything slipping, knowing he'd already spoken foolishly, saying things he didn't exactly believe. He didn't think it was good for people to do things they didn't want to do, simply for the sake of it. Life was more complicated than that. "Colorado stretches you," he tried again, "because it's different from where you are the rest of the year."

"Yeah. It's backward."

He tried to think of the right thing to say, but all he could think was that when Camille came she would meet Leah, and Leah was pregnant with his baby. And only child Camille did not like small children. She wouldn't like Mary Grace, and she wouldn't like the baby. She would spend eight weeks doing her best to make everyone's life miserable.

I have to keep that from happening. Was there any concession he could offer her, something that might make Colorado slightly more appealing to her? "Camille, would you like to have a friend out to visit while you're here?"

"I don't want to come at all. Dad, I'm getting another call. I've got to go."

"Can we talk later in the week?"

A sigh. "Yeah. Let me get this call. Goodbye, okay?"

"Take care, Camille. I love you."

She said nothing more, just hung up. After a moment, Mark followed suit.

Then, he stood to close the blinds of his Ouray apartment, to shut out the spring night. He'd always thought his house, the house on the Dallas Divide, would be a fun place for his daughter to come, a place for her to experience adventure and know something different from her life in California. He took her bike riding, camping, hiking, though it was like pulling teeth to take her anywhere that involved being out of cell-phone range. He kept telling himself that the summer visits *did* matter and *would* matter, would influence who she eventually became.

But it didn't seem to be helping. Camille was becoming more shallow with each passing year. He'd had another appointment with a counselor who had reminded him that Camille was young, that the priorities she had as a teenager were not necessarily those she would adopt as an adult.

If only she lived with him, instead of with Sabrina and Bill. Bill was an agent for Hollywood actors, actresses and writers. Sabrina did not work. Mark was unable to pinpoint one aspect of that lifestyle which was good for his daughter. But he'd signed his rights away years earlier. Phone calls, eight weeks in summer and seven days in winter, were what he had.

And this summer Camille would meet Leah and Mary Grace. Mark wanted them to be part of his family. He wanted the baby Leah carried to have two parents in the home, parents committed to each other in love and fidelity. But Leah seemed unwilling to commit to that sort of future with him, dismissing his feelings. She'd told him in so many words that she thought it would be foolish for them to marry or even live together for the sake of the child.

And he still had not told his daughter or her mother that Camille would soon have a half brother or half sister.

Laguna Beach, California
Camille's journal

Dear Diary,

James called! He just wanted to know if I wanted to go down and look at the tide pools with him. He said we have to get up at six in the morning! I guess it's kind of like a date. Maybe we'll get coffee or something afterward. He wants to draw some of the tide-pool animals for Biology class. Whatever.

Sheri Stern got her belly button redone. She had an outie and wanted it fixed. Fortunately, I don't have to worry about that. She says she's posing for lots of photos for her boyfriend, and they're putting them on the Internet. There's a contest where people can win free boob jobs. Fortunately, my parents will pay for mine. I'm going to ask Mom if I can just get it done in the last two weeks of school. After all, I can do home school, and there's nothing that important at the end of the year. Then I can recover in Colorado. I know she'll say yes. She knows how important it is to me.

Chapter Five

The second Saturday after May Day, Mark called Leah to say he would be down later in the day to start sanding and prepping her house to paint. Leah and Mary Grace spent the morning in the garden, uprooting bindweed and unwelcome thistles. The garden area to the side of the house was roughly the size of a private swimming pool. It was free of the scourges that still fought to regain hold elsewhere on the property—Russian thistle, knapweed, cheatgrass—the introduced banes of the Western landholder. She and Sam had dedicated themselves to stamping out these intruders without herbicides—a tall order. And, taking care of the property alone in the three years since Sam's death, Leah had gradually lost ground in the battle. Every year she pulled, chopped, suffocated the bad weeds, whichever the individual species demanded, then sowed rice grass and Western wheatgrass. But it was backbreaking work for one person.

Nonetheless, she loved spring, loved to grow things, to put out the plants she'd nurtured from seedlings in her solarium.

"How long till our baby comes?" Mary Grace asked Leah as she did every day.

"About the time the zinnias bloom," Leah replied as she did every day. "Just when the corn is sweetest." She looked out past the row of cottonwoods along the irrigation ditch, past other trees edging the south side of the property, toward the snow-dappled mountains. Mark's world.

He'd also mentioned talking to someone in Paonia about a job in the area for the summer months. He would leave someone else in charge of his business, he had explained, if he found work in Paonia.

Leah was nervous, nervous that he had claimed to be falling in love with her, nervous about the possibility of his moving to Paonia. Most of all, she was nervous about the rush of pleasure she felt whenever she heard his voice on the phone, which was at least once a day.

Mary Grace tramped along a row to look at the zinnia plants. She wore her "fairy dress," a pink and purple velvet and net ballerina-style dress that was a hand-me-down from the daughter of one of Leah's friends. Would the child she carried be a girl or a boy? She had no preference, wondered if Mark would and somehow doubted it.

Of course, Mark was feeling so much tension over his daughter's wish for breast implants. Leah had no good advice to offer him on the subject, only hoped that Mary Grace would grow up with unassailable self-confidence and not feel the need to change her body so as to fit in with the expectations of others, whether male or female.

She heard Mark's truck, and she walked around the side of the house to greet him. She was wearing her favorite maternity dress, one a friend had picked up in Hawaii. It was royal blue with a batik pattern in turquoise and was embellished with brass I Ching coins. Her arms and back were bare, and the spring sun beating down on her skin was warm and soothing.

Mark climbed out of his vehicle, stretched and seemed to take a moment to appreciate the beauty of the day. He tilted his face up to study the sky, then the leaves of the oaks and cottonwoods near the irrigation ditch and shading the grassy front yard.

Leah had spent hours the evening before deciding whether or not to insist upon paying Mark for painting the house. In the end, she'd decided that she would let him do it as a gift to his child—not to her. She intended to explain this to him but wasn't sure how to go about it. What she knew with certainty was that men could interpret favors done as payment for favors to come to them. She didn't want to owe Mark Logan—or any other man—any favors.

She walked across the lawn toward him. "Good morning."

"Hi." He scrutinized the front of her house before moving toward the back of his truck to remove an aluminum extension ladder and other tools.

Leah's heart thudded. The roof. She'd forgotten that he would have to be up on a ladder.

She hadn't been home when Sam had fallen. He and River had been working together. River had called 911, knowing it was too late, because Sam had broken his neck in the fall, had been dead when River reached his side.

"I don't—I don't want you doing this," she said.

"What?"

"I—I'll pay someone. Someone else."

Mark gazed down at her, then seemed to understand. "I'm good on ladders," he said.

"So was Sam." Though Sam had been on the roof, not on a ladder, at the time.

She felt and saw Mark searching her face, her eyes. Finally he gave a small sigh and said, "Tell you what. I'll start with the prep work I can do from the ground. I'll get scaffolding and some other guys to help me with whatever we do above ground."

Leah's jaw was clenched tight. She made herself relax. "All right."

INSIDE, she made lunch for herself and Mark and Mary Grace. Mary Grace was outside hand-sanding the steps—helping Mark. Leah was glad for the solitude. It had shaken her when she'd realized she cared about Mark getting up on a ladder, that the thought of his falling as Sam had frightened her.

It struck her as strange, because the way she'd most experienced Sam's death was as a loss of security. She'd been horrified by her own reaction. Her first thought had been, *Now I have to do it all alone.* Take care of the property, raise Mary Grace, earn a living.

Having learned to cope without her husband, she was reluctant to become dependent on someone again. Not only that. Mark Logan was intelligent, attractive and steady, but she sensed he was also strong-willed and knew, by his admission, that he could adopt a rigid point of view. Though Mary Grace seemed to like him, the four-year-old wasn't yet in the position of having to answer to him as she would to a father. Many of Mark's notions, Leah sensed, came from ideology rather than practicality.

She sat down at the piano to play and sing, opening one of her Joni Mitchell books.

She'd been practicing for ten minutes when her phone rang. She hurried to pick up the cordless handset, checking the caller ID from habit. Her client Dusty was due in two weeks. Even as she saw Dusty's number in the small window, Leah foresaw taking Mary Grace across town to the woman who always took care of her when Leah was called to births. Once upon a time, Leah had thought it would be natural and make sense to pay Ellen to take care of Mary Grace. But the fact was, Ellen was always busy with Ellen's needs. When Ellen had first confided her desire to have a child, Leah had said, "You don't even like children!" Ellen had been hurt, and maybe her hurt was why Leah had agreed to become a surrogate mother for her sister.

"You're always judging me," Ellen had said. "You know, I am a responsible adult. I've accomplished a lot in my life, even if I didn't do it all the Leah Williams way."

Leah answered the phone. "Hi, Dusty. What's up?"

"Leah, I've got this cramping. And I think I might have lost the mucus plug this morning. I saw something that might have been the mucus plug."

"I'll come over and have a look," Leah said. "Is Jim there?"

"Well, not this second, but he knows what's going on. He took Aaron over to Jodie's."

The same place Leah would take Mary Grace.

"All right. I'll be there in a half hour," Leah said, "and we'll see where you are."

As she hurried into her bedroom to change, then began putting together what Mary Grace might need for as many as forty-eight hours away from her mother, Leah thought again of Mark Logan's concern for his daughter. Obviously, he took fatherhood seriously. She should count herself lucky that the father of the child she carried now actually seemed to *care* about his responsibilities. But she remembered too keenly the conflicts of marriage, not conflicts out of the ordinary but those that were part and parcel of the institution.

I'm not going to marry Mark Logan, in any case.

She went out on the porch. Mary Grace had stopped helping with sanding and was playing with two of her stuffed animals under the oak tree, having a picnic with them, using her doll-size teacups and plates, with rocks and sticks for food.

Mark was running a power sander, but as she stepped outside, Leah caught him turning to check on Mary Grace, to see where the four-year-old was and what she was doing. He turned off the sander when he saw Leah, and when the sound had died away Leah told him that she needed to check on a client who might be in labor.

"Would you like me to watch Mary Grace?" he asked.

Leah shook her head. "She goes to Jodie Simon's. It's our routine. If this *is* actually labor, I could be there forty-eight hours."

"Or more?"

She said, "Not many moms want to stick it out past then, and I like to be careful. I've only had a couple of labors go longer than that in a home setting."

"And probably fewer in a clinic or hospital," he said, sounding grim.

Leah sensed again that ideological rigidity in him. She agreed that too often women giving birth in hospitals faced a rather unforgiving clock. Dilate so many centimeters in so many hours or we'll do a cesarean section. But she could picture Mark Logan, perhaps for the best of reasons, pressuring the mother of his child to stick out a difficult labor for five days if it meant the result was natural childbirth. And now Leah was the mother of his child.

Why do I keep seeing him as idealistic to a fault?

But she didn't, not really. She just felt…cautious.

Now, he said, "That must be hard on Mary Grace."

"She likes going to Jodie's," Leah told him. "Jodie has been sitting for her all her life." *Of course, it's hard for Mary Grace,* she thought. Did Mark think she should have given up midwifery, lived on Social Security from Sam's death, so that Mary Grace would never have to spend a night apart from her? She hated herself for saying *anything* more about the matter. Yet she couldn't remain silent. "I suppose you think that's bad mothering?"

"No." But the accusation didn't seem to wound him;

it didn't even seem to come as unexpected, as though maybe her question *did* reflect his feelings. "I'm just— surprised, I suppose. It seems like she'd be happier at Ellen's."

"You don't know my sister," Leah muttered.

"You and I both thought she'd make a good mother."

Or the pregnancy would never have happened, Leah reflected. "Mary Grace," she called. "I have a birth. Ready to go to Jodie's?"

Mary Grace gave her a stubborn look, one Leah recognized. Her daughter was going to pick a fight, refuse to go to Jodie's—or try to.

"I don't want to go," Mary Grace said. "I'll stay here with Mark."

"No, you won't," Leah said.

Mary Grace turned back to her tea party.

Leah felt herself flush. Was anything more embarrassing than her child misbehaving in front of a guest? That Mary Grace did it so seldom and that Mark was something more than a guest just made it more excruciating.

Mark had put down the sander. He gazed across the yard at Mary Grace, but, thankfully, he didn't offer again that Mary Grace could stay with him. That would have worked toward rewarding her disobedience. Leah noted that he seemed content to observe the coming conflict.

Leah marched over the lawn. "Mary Grace, pick up Turtle and Snoops and come inside to get ready to go to Jodie's. I want you to change, and you need to pick out any toys you want to bring."

"I don't want to go to Jodie's." Mary Grace didn't look up at her but sat on the lawn with a determined frown on her face.

"I'm sorry, but this is what we have to do, so that I can help at Dusty's birth."

"Why can't I go with you to Dusty's?"

"Aaron's not even going to be there. He'll be at Jodie's, too."

"Oh." Slowly, without looking up at her mother, Mary Grace gathered up her two stuffed friends and the tea dishes. She walked inside with a sulky expression, never glancing at Mark.

Leah allowed herself a small breath of relief. She said, "There's a bed in my office inside. You can spend the night in there if it's easier for you."

"Thanks," he said. "I might take you up on that." Then, he said, "I liked listening to you."

It took her a moment to realize that he had heard her playing the piano and singing.

"Thank you," she said.

Now, Leah imagined Mark Logan alone in her house that night, imagined herself coming home in the small hours, knowing he was asleep in her office.

Well, there was no telling when she'd be home from Dusty's.

To TELL *Camille now or later?* Mark wondered yet again.

Late that afternoon, twisting the cap from a beer as he sat on the sanded porch, he opened his cell phone to call his daughter.

"Hi, this is Camille's cell phone. Leave a message if you like."

"Hi, Camille. It's Dad. Just wondering how you're doing and if your friend Tish is going to be able to come with you this summer. I did leave a message for her mom, but I haven't gotten a call back. I hope you're having a good day, and I love you. Talk to you soon."

He shut the phone. The news about Leah and the baby certainly wasn't the kind of thing he was going to impart through a recorded message.

In person. Maybe when he picked her up from the airport. Yes, that would be better, telling her face-to-face. *Well, I just donated my sperm, but your uncle River and aunt Ellen changed their minds.* It would all sound so crazy.

Not the kind of decision he'd want to see Camille making, now or in the future.

Not to mention that it was a huge surprise to spring on his daughter when she reached Colorado. No, he'd have to find a way to tell her over the phone. But what if she found the news disturbing enough that she would refuse to come? Yes, he could contact a judge to try to enforce the visitation, but that would bring Camille into the courtroom, where she could tell a judge that she didn't want to visit her father.

Of course, she could refuse to come as things were, but he didn't think Sabrina would support that. He sensed Sabrina enjoyed those weeks without Camille.

He considered calling Leah to see how the birth was going. Maybe she'd need an errand run. A laboring woman didn't need the midwife in the room every minute.

He pushed the number 2 on his phone, the number he had programmed as Leah's, which required some shuffling. Camille 1. Leah 2. River, his business, the rest of his life, following.

"Hello?"

He hadn't expected her to pick up. Her voice affected him as it always did, with a pleasurable warmth caressing his skin. He pictured her beautiful face with its fine angular bones and almost translucent skin. "It's Mark."

"Is everything all right?" she asked.

"Yes. Yes. I just—wanted to check how it's going over there."

"Fine," she said in a way that made him think there was a much bigger story she wasn't free to reveal.

"I wanted to let you know, if you need me to bring you anything… Well, I'm here."

"Thanks. Thanks. I have what I need just now. Thank you, though."

"You're welcome. I'll let you go."

"Fine. Thanks again," she said and hung up.

DUSTY WAS progressing slowly and unevenly. Leah forced herself to relax with the pace. One advantage of a home birth was that no one pressured the mother to reach a certain stage of labor by a particular time. The parameters that defined normal labor were so broad and varied that Leah had taught herself to accept many speeds of labor and patterns of progress as "normal."

"Do you want to break the bag of waters?" Dusty asked when Leah reentered her bedroom after ending her conversation with Mark.

"It's not necessary at this point," Leah said. "You're doing beautifully." She'd been checking the baby's heartbeat regularly with a fetoscope.

Dusty's partner, Jim, sat beside her on their big four-poster bed, in the afternoon sunlight streaming into the loft where they slept. Their home was an A-frame on the edge of town with a good-size garden. Jim and Dusty both worked as graphic artists, specializing in Web site design.

"Do you think I should stand up during contractions?" Dusty said. "Would that help?"

"I think you should do what feels best for you," Leah said.

"I want to take a shower."

"Great idea. Let me help you."

Over the next two hours, Dusty got in and out of the shower many times. Jim brought a plastic chair into the shower stall so that his wife could hold on to it, bending over it as the warm water sprayed down her skin.

"Five centimeters," Leah told her. "You're doing great. It won't be long now."

Dusty didn't answer, just stepped into the shower again, moaning as she held the chair.

MARK BLINKED awake, realizing abruptly that he was in unfamiliar surroundings. It was dawn, and he heard quiet sounds from the other side of the office door. Leah was home.

He slid silently from the spare bed in his sweatpants and dragged a white T-shirt over his head. Then he went to the door and opened it.

She had an unearthly glow to her in that blue dress she'd been wearing earlier with a navy cardigan over it.

She glanced toward the door and smiled.

He wanted to touch the curves of her face. She was the most exquisite woman. But she was busy putting things away in the kitchen, food she must have taken to the birth with her.

"Sleep all right?" she asked. Her eyes fell on his guitar case, near the couch where he'd left it the night before. "You play?" she said before he could answer her first question.

"Yes. Tell me about the birth."

That smile again, a wide arc of a smile revealing small straight teeth, very white. "Girl. Alicia Anne. Six pounds seven ounces. Or do you want the blow-by-blow?"

"Actually, yes." He moved to the kitchen door frame and paused there, waiting.

She pulled out a chair from the table and sank into it.

He didn't sit across from her but said, "Can I get you anything? Breakfast?"

"I just had half a grapefruit and some yogurt."

So he joined her at the table, and she told him about the birth, about the way labor had progressed and the fact that Alicia Anne had been born with a cawl over her head, intact.

When she had finished, Mark reached across the table, laying his hand on hers. Her fingers were smooth, white, delicate. He hadn't been intimate with a woman for three years. A series of girlfriends unwilling to commit to him and his lifestyle had made him bitter about romance. What he felt for Leah seemed distinctly different from those earlier encounters. And he wouldn't allow himself to think that his relationship with her would just be another verse of the same song—unwillingness to make a permanent commitment. But her fingers were motionless beneath his.

It did not fool him, because suddenly he could see the pulse in her throat, see it thrumming hard and fast.

He wanted to kiss her, but he *didn't* want to take advantage of her, to put her in a position where necessity or convenience won her for him.

He released her hand.

Across from him, Leah tucked her own hand beneath the table. She'd found herself staring at his jaw, at the blond hair sweeping across his forehead and curling at his collar. It occurred to her that Mark was more handsome, more physically perfect and perhaps more compatible with her than any man she'd ever known.

She'd loved Sam, yes, but since his death she'd become someone different. In Sam she'd chosen safe stability—and it had failed her. Mark Logan was enigmatic; Leah felt that she could know him for years and never reach his depths. She also sensed his attraction to her. Being a midwife, however, she understood how a man's heart and desire could be influenced by the fact of a woman carrying his child.

She made herself say, "Mark, it's just that I'm carrying your child. If I weren't—well, you would probably never even have taken me to lunch."

"You think?" He didn't seem to be actually asking. Rather, his eyes watched her lips, roved over her face. She felt him inspecting her, and the look was as a caress.

She stood. "And it's time for me to catch a couple of hours' sleep before I pick up Mary Grace."

"Would you like me to go get her?"

She hesitated. She'd have to tell Jodie that he was coming; Jodie wouldn't let someone she didn't know take Mary Grace, even if Mary Grace knew the person. She and Leah had a strict understanding about that.

"Maybe another time," she said. "Thank you, though."

Laguna Beach, California
Camille's journal

Dear Diary,

Dr. Henderson said he wouldn't do the surgery if I was going to be traveling to Colorado so soon afterward. I'm really bummed. Also, James hasn't called me again since we went to the tide pools. I can't figure out what I did wrong. Tish says he's been hanging out with Lissa, that nerd! Also, he told Scott he thinks the girls here are all shallow. Thanks, James. I asked Tish if she thinks I'm shallow, and she says no and pointed out that I keep this journal and like to write and stuff. Also, I have the weird father in Colorado who lives without connection to electricity or water, everything solar and from the well. Maybe I should have talked to James about that. But I don't think it's that cool. I think it's inconvenient. My phone doesn't even work right up there.

Dad says Tish can come visit me in Colorado and stay for a few weeks, but even that seems depressing. All the guys will like her because she has such a fabulous body. I really don't want to go. What if I get sick or go on a hunger strike? There has to be some way I can get out of going.

Chapter Six

"Is Mark going to be my daddy?" Mary Grace asked.

Leah was driving her daughter home from preschool. Mark would not be there. He and two of his friends had finished painting the house in the colors Leah had chosen—a rich ivory with tile-red trim. Mark had not spent more than that one night in her spare room, and Leah had been glad for that. She was attracted to him, but she couldn't escape the feeling that he was watching her and Mary Grace—watching and judging.

Mary Grace apparently hadn't noticed.

Leah was slow to answer her daughter. *Sam is your daddy.*

Well, yes.

Do you want Mark to be your daddy?

All wrong. Mary Grace should not necessarily be asked her opinion on such a subject.

No. How about that answer, Leah? *No, Mark is not going to be your daddy.* She ought to be able to speak those words.

So Leah said, "Well, he's the new baby's daddy."

"I don't like Mark," Mary Grace announced.

"Why not?" This was something Leah hadn't anticipated.

"He wouldn't let me finish singing."

Leah remembered the scene vividly. Mark and Leah had been sitting at the table looking at paint chips. Mary Grace had entered the kitchen in her turquoise princess dress and had begun to sing an aria, at the top of her lungs.

Mark had said, "Mary Grace, your mom and I are talking. You need to be quiet now."

In return, Mary Grace had announced that she was the Queen Stardust and the house was *her* castle, and *he* needed to be quiet and listen to *her*.

Leah had been charmed by her daughter. Mary Grace was embracing an archetype, expressing her being.

Mark, on the other hand, had assumed an authority that she, Leah, had not granted him. He'd said, "Wrong. It's your mother's castle, and she and I are having a conversation. If you need to sing, go in your bedroom."

Mary Grace had said, "It's not *your* castle."

Leah also remembered the argument that had followed, out of Mary Grace's earshot, between Mark and herself. She hadn't disciplined or corrected Mary Grace, and Mark had found fault with that.

"Any other reasons?" she now asked Mary Grace.

"He thinks he's the boss."

"In what way?"

"He sends me to my room."

Mark had yet to send Mary Grace to her room. He'd once told her to go there, and Leah had told him that wasn't his place.

She hadn't been comfortable with that decision but would have been less comfortable letting him prevail. To let him prevail would have meant that she *did* want him around, that she accepted the role he'd appointed himself in her life, both hers and Mary Grace's. Out of her daughter's earshot, she'd told him, "It's not your place to discipline her."

He'd said, "How are you going to let go and allow me a part in parenting *our* child?"

Good question. She couldn't very well have different rules for Mary Grace and the new baby.

She'd said, "You make the rules at your house. I make the rules at mine." End of subject—for that time.

She'd grown used to doing things her own way. And her way worked. Mary Grace was assertive, spirited, self-confident, sure of who she was. True, she wasn't always respectful to adults, including Leah. But it wasn't from any sense of badness—and it definitely wasn't obnoxious.

"Are you going to marry Mark?" Mary Grace asked now.

"What?" Leah asked, startled. She turned the car carefully into her own driveway.

"I don't want you to marry him."

"Why not?" Leah asked.

"I want it to be just the two of us," Mary Grace said. "I don't want anyone else."

"There's going to be a new baby," Leah told her as

she parked outside the house, feeling a strange emptiness at *not* seeing Mark's truck there, even though it was what she'd expected.

Even though it was what she'd told herself was best.

"I'll take care of the baby," Mary Grace said. Without waiting for her mother's response, she climbed out of her car seat by herself and ran to the house, happy to be home and filled with her own plans.

Leah replayed the conversation her daughter had started about Mark just as her cell phone rang. She answered it as she followed Mary Grace up the newly painted front steps.

"Leah, it's Ellen. I'm bleeding again."

Leah's heart seemed to clench and unclench. If Ellen miscarried… She didn't even want to consider it. She didn't want to have to say to her sister that the baby in Leah's womb was no longer waiting in reserve for Ellen.

She had been planning to lie down for a few minutes while Mary Grace began her post-preschool activities, probably starting some game with her dolls or stuffed animals, a game she would interrupt for lunch. Now, as she reached the door, a knifelike pain cut through her hip and groin area on her right leg. It was so excruciating that for a moment she clung to the front doorjamb, standing on the opposite leg, willing the pain to subside.

She knew what it was of course, had experienced it during her pregnancy with Mary Grace. Sciatica. That damned nerve the diameter of her pinky. She swore softly then spoke unevenly to her sister. "Tell me what's happening. When did it start?"

"I noticed it just now when I went to the bathroom. And I'm cramping."

"I'll be over as soon as I can get there. I just have to get Mary Grace back in the car."

Too much, too much, too much, drummed her mind as she put her phone back in her carryall and called her daughter's name. *Ow, ow, ow.* It was pain that could make her throw up, sudden debilitating pain. She needed to lie down, to try some yoga postures to ease pressure on the nerve. She sat down in the doorway.

"What is it, Mommy?" asked Mary Grace, the picture of a good child, beautiful and concerned, someone self-confident in her own being.

How Leah loved her. She said, "Sweetie, I'm so sorry, but that was Aunt Ellen. She's having some problems with her pregnancy, and it's very important we go over there. Can you pick some toys quickly and come?"

"Yes. Why are you sitting down?"

"I have sciatica. I'll tell you about it in the car. It's nothing bad—it just hurts." *Saint-John's-wort.* The tincture had worked wonders during her pregnancy with Mary Grace. It didn't work for everyone, but it had helped Leah. *Please work this time, too.* Her midwifery bag was in the car, and there should be some Saint-John's-wort in it.

The day was already warming up. She would have liked to change out of the long-sleeved cotton maternity dress she'd put on to pick up Mary Grace from preschool, but she didn't want to walk any more than necessary until this excruciating pain stopped.

"Can I kiss it?" Mary Grace asked, the willing mother's helper.

Enchanted, squeezing her daughter against her, Leah lifted her face for a kiss. "You can kiss me. Yes."

How much easier it would have been if Mark were there, if she could just leave Mary Grace with him. *But he'd be working anyhow, Leah. He wouldn't be home when you needed him for something like this.*

Not to mention that Mark's work was in the San Juan Mountains to the south. It was not in Paonia.

But as she readied to go to Ellen's, she continued thinking about her practice—and the changes the new baby would bring. How was she going to keep her practice going when she had a new infant to care for and no assistant? She had taken on apprentices and assistants in the past, but none had lasted very long. They were women who thought they wanted to be midwives but then changed their minds when faced with being present at twenty-four-hour labors. Leah was able to nap during long births, and her personal biorhythms seemed designed for this career. Not everyone was so fortunate.

Leah told herself firmly that this was one more problem that Mark Logan's presence in her life was not going to solve. So she should stop thinking about him so much.

"Mark, this is Jason Adams." The very young proprietor of the business in Paonia with which Mark had interviewed. Mark was at the coffeehouse in Ouray, Uncommon Grounds, when his cell phone rang.

"Yes, Jason. It's good to hear from you." And it was. Jason Adams owned a business called Wilderness Challenge, which ran programs for juvenile offenders, taking them out on the Uncompahgre Plateau, Grand Mesa and the Gunnison River. Wilderness Challenge operated from Paonia and this particular offer came with a small house. Mark's only hesitation, in fact, was that to him Jason seemed a person with little empathy, concerned mostly with accumulating a long résumé of "sick" climbs in South America and elsewhere during the weeks of the year when he could be away from the office. In fact, Jason's purpose in hiring Mark would be to allow him the freedom for as much globetrotting as possible. But Mark believed in the business.

"We're willing to try you out, Mark, considering that you have backcountry experience and a masters and have owned your own business."

Mark's university background was in sports and fitness and psychology. He'd skied competitively and had planned, back then, to work as a coach. So the job opening with Wilderness Challenge for someone to oversee counselors and clients, to interface with families and run the show when Jason was gone was cut out for him. "Thank you," he answered Jason.

"I'm really looking for someone who will be able to understand the business," Jason said. "Like I said, someone who can handle any crisis."

Mark said nothing. Jason knew his qualifications, and they'd discussed all this.

"When can you start?" Jason asked.

"Any time." He had a reliable manager in Ouray, a solid employee willing to assume greater responsibility for more money.

It was time for him to start trying to fit into Paonia. Because the baby Leah Williams was carrying was his child. And Leah was his family, too, whether she knew it yet or not.

"ELLEN, let's talk about you seeing Dr. Holmes." Leah's backup physician in Delta was the man to whom she referred high-risk clients.

"I want to have this baby at home."

Leah's tension, sciatica and general frustration weren't helped by the fact that Danine and Astra were at Ellen's house. Though Mary Grace and Astra had gone outside to play together and weren't yet fighting, Leah suspected that a conflict was probably in the offing. Astra was a demanding playmate, and Mary Grace did not take well to being bossed by friends.

Worse, Danine was sitting on Ellen's bed with her. She said, "You need to respect Ellen's wishes. She's the mother."

Leah said, "And I'm her midwife. I also hope that Ellen can have her baby at home, but I'd like her to—"

"Babies."

Leah blinked.

Danine sat forward slightly, eyes and complexion glowing. "Twins. I feel their souls."

Leah thought Danine Luce was a fraud and wanted nothing more than to order her out of the house. But this was Ellen's house, and Danine was Ellen's friend.

Ellen was gazing at Danine with a wondrous expression that made Leah want to throw up.

"I'd like you to have an ultrasound," Leah said. "And at some point you must have an appointment with Dr. Holmes anyhow. That's what my agreement with him is."

"I think Ellen should be able to make her own choice for the lives of these children," said Danine, holding Ellen's hand.

Leah had listened to her sister's womb with the fetoscope. Supposing Danine's preposterous prognostication was true, it would have been very difficult to detect the heartbeats of two fetuses at this stage. And yet... Leah reviewed the figures she'd just written in Ellen's chart. The weight gain. Not abnormal, but high for Ellen's overall size.

Well, if Danine happened to be right, Dr. Holmes could tell Ellen that her pregnancy was high-risk. Life was high-risk, no guarantees. But some pregnancies should be followed by obstetricians and should take place in hospital settings. It was too soon to say if that should be the case for Ellen. The bleeding, however, was cause for concern.

She said, "You need to rest, Ellen. Really take it easy. I know how hard that is for you, but I mean it. Try staying in bed and getting up only to go to the bathroom. And I'll let Dr. Holmes's office know that you need an appointment." She had brewed an infusion for Ellen, one she hoped would keep her sister from miscarrying.

"Can you deliver twins at home?" Ellen asked.

We don't know it's twins. "I doubt you're carrying twins." Leah cast an apologetic smile toward Danine. In any case, Ellen had asked something she couldn't answer. Leah herself never spoke of "delivering" babies but of attending births. If midwifery had taught her anything, it was that the laboring woman did the work. Now she said, "I've never attended the home birth of twins, but let's not borrow trouble—or babies. In any case, you need to be followed by a physician, Ellen. Especially because of the spotting."

Her sister, whose hair was the same shade as Leah's but very curly, looked up at Leah with her dark eyes. Leah knew that for Ellen, with her alternative lifestyle, submitting to a hospital birth would feel like some sort of failure. Leah had encountered this attitude in clients before, and she hadn't yet found a way to make a woman who was set on a home birth content with a hospital birth. Only the pregnant woman herself could do that.

To Leah, the choice to go to the hospital if she or the baby she carried was in trouble during the birth was a fairly simple one. It had not happened with Mary Grace's birth, but if there had been problems that could be better dealt with in a hospital environment, that's where she would have gone. Now, because Ellen was her sister, she found herself saying something she would not have said to another client. "Don't you think it's more important that you and the baby get the right care?" *Priorities, Ellen! Priorities!* she wanted to shout.

"I don't know. I think maybe it's the most important thing to let nature take its course."

"That's wisdom," Danine said, stroking Ellen's brow.

Ellen cast a look of gratitude at the wing nut, as Leah had begun to think of her. *God, don't let Ellen invite this woman to the birth.*

Leah said, "Danine, I'd like a few minutes to speak privately with Ellen."

Danine lifted her head, her posture excellent, queenly, with her Michelle Pfeiffer beauty. "Of course," she said. "I'll check on our girls." She leaned gracefully forward to kiss Ellen's forehead, then slipped off the bed and out of the room, silently closing the door behind her.

When she had gone, Leah said, "Ellen, if you'd adopted the baby I'm carrying, it might have happened that I had to go to the hospital. Labor doesn't come with many guarantees."

"But you wouldn't have gone to the hospital," Ellen said.

"I *will* go if I must," Leah corrected her.

"But if it was our baby—"

Leah came face-to-face with her own culpability in assuming the pregnancy that was now such a fact of her life. Why had she never thought to have this conversation with Ellen earlier? It was moot now, of course. And Leah thought it wise to stress this. "Well, it doesn't matter, because I'm keeping this baby."

"Even if—"

Leah cut her off with a sense of disbelief. "Yes," she said. "You made your choice." She didn't want to think about a scenario in which Ellen lost her pregnancy. The bitterness that might result... And Leah wouldn't be willing to go through this again for her sister. "Mark and I are both committed to parenting this child," she said firmly.

Ellen sipped the infusion that should stop her cramping and the bleeding. Trying to ignore the tension following her own announcement, Leah made notes for her sister and for River, a plan to follow to help ward off a miscarriage. Foregoing sexual intercourse for a while, some bed rest for Ellen, which would be a challenge for her sister, who liked to be up and about, active.

"Are you and Mark going to be together?" Ellen asked.

The question hadn't been asked in a challenging way, yet Leah felt defensive. "I don't know," she said and changed the subject. "I'm going to call Dr. Holmes and let him know I'm referring you. As I said, you have to go to his office in any case. All of my clients go through an introductory exam with him. That's part of my agreement with him."

"Financial incentive," Ellen said.

Leah stared. "No. That has nothing to do with it. He makes very little money from my clients. It's so that he is as sure as I am that a client is a good candidate for home birth."

"His way of getting us into the system."

Leah's temper frayed to the breaking point. "Not everything is a conspiracy, Ellen." She took a deep breath. It had to be said. "Look, you're free to choose a different care provider. You could go to Kassandra."

"She won't take someone with twins. She's too afraid of things she can't control."

This was not Leah's view of her own midwife. What she said was, "You're not carrying twins." She didn't know this for an absolute fact, just knew it was unlikely. "And just because I'm your sister, that doesn't make me the right birth attendant for you. In fact, it might make me less good for you and River."

Her cell phone rang. It was in her purse, now lying with her midwifery bag on a chair near the bed. Leah turned away from her sister to check the number. Mark. She'd let him leave a message while she finished with Ellen.

Ten minutes later, after Ellen had agreed to a consultation with Dr. Holmes, Leah sat in her sister's kitchen and listened to Mark's message.

"You told me that you're taking Mary Grace to Delta on Saturday. Camille's coming that day, I'd like you to meet. Any chance of my driving you to Delta? Then I'll continue on to Montrose to meet her at the airport. That will give Camille and me a chance to talk. Then we could pick you up and drive you home on the way to the base house. Which is also my way of saying I'm now working for Wilderness Challenge."

The base house was only half a mile from Leah's place, accessible via a dirt road with little traffic, but Leah, as a long-time Paonia resident, was well aware of the building's drawbacks, which she'd gently detailed to Mark.

Rustic, he'd agreed, but free rent was free rent. And the office of Wilderness Challenge was next door.

Leah wished ruefully to be either of an innocent age

or perhaps simply to be like Ellen and not be the kind of woman who would weigh all the pros and cons of the invitation to be part of the ride home from the airport. *Mark is trying to make us a family.*

But was he? As much as he seemed attracted to her, she continued to see him as watching her mothering of Mary Grace with a critical eye.

For her, that was a red light, reminding her how much easier it was to live in a world where she made the rules.

But it was lonelier, too.

I'm attracted to this man. If truth be told, profoundly attracted, more attracted than she'd ever been to another man. Yet her life as a midwife had made her disciplined, cautious, careful.

She played the message again. She would go back to the bedroom in fifteen minutes, see how Ellen was feeling. She'd already left a message for Dr. Holmes.

How would Camille Logan feel about meeting Leah? If Mark chose to break the news that he was going to be a father again as soon as her plane landed, that wouldn't give her much time to process the information before meeting Leah.

Leah pushed the number she'd programmed into the phone for him. It was 9, replacing the number of a friend who'd moved and whose new number was programmed as 30.

"Hi, Leah."

"Hi, Mark." Of course, he'd recognized her number. "How will your daughter feel about that?" she said without preamble. "I mean, you're springing a lot on her. Don't you think it would be best to give her more time to take it all in?"

There was a pause and she imagined him rubbing one strong, long-fingered hand along his jaw, something she'd seen him do when he was thinking something over. "You could be right," he said at last. "But I don't think it's going to make much difference."

"Don't shortchange your daughter," Leah said.

"She's likely to be in Paonia when the baby is born, Leah. And I want that. Even if you don't feel comfortable with her being present—"

"I'm not sure I feel that way," Leah said. "I haven't met her, but I imagine I'll like her."

His laugh was short and rueful. "Thank goodness for that hope. Are you busy tonight? I'm moving some things down to the house."

He was going to come back to Paonia tonight. But stay in his own place. Nonetheless, her heart beat more quickly. "No."

"Want company?"

"Thank you," she said. "Yes. I'll make something fun for dinner, if you want to eat with us."

"Just tell me when."

LEAH DRESSED with care that evening in a flowing raw-silk maternity dress. She worked barefoot in the kitchen, cutting vegetables and cubing tofu for a stir-fry.

Mary Grace had wanted to use the opportunity to wear her favorite purple dress, which was like a smaller version of Leah's. She hadn't complained about Mark coming to dinner, and Leah hoped her daughter had said all she planned to say on the subject of not liking Mark. No. That wasn't true. She hoped that Mary Grace *would* like him. At first, it had seemed as though she did like him.

"Is Mark going to sleep over?" she asked as she took the orange juice out of the refrigerator to pour herself a cup.

Leah hovered nearby, wanting to encourage Mary Grace's self-reliance yet not in the mood to clean up a spill.

Mary Grace managed the task perfectly, until she put the carton back in the refrigerator and it began to tip.

Leah caught it before it could fall and slid it back into place on the shelf.

"I don't think so," Leah said. "He has his own house now." Mark had slept in the spare room a few times now. The thought of him sleeping in her room, sharing her bed, made her flush.

Sleeping with him would be the beginning of a commitment. She was a mother, and that role dictated so much of her behavior. Sharing herself physically with a man could never be casual for her—for Mary Grace's sake, as well as her own.

"Oh," Mary Grace said. "Does he like stories?"

"I don't know. Most people like stories," Leah said. "Don't you think?"

"Is he going to be my new daddy?"

That question again, the question to which Leah had not said no and found she could not say no. "I don't know, Mary Grace."

"He's not going to live with us," Mary Grace said, "so I guess not."

Leah decided again to try to learn Mary Grace's precise feelings toward Mark. "Wouldn't that be okay?" she asked. "If he became part of our family?"

"No," Mary Grace said firmly.

"Why not?" Leah asked. Mark and Mary Grace had never been alone together, which meant Leah had observed every encounter between the two of them. As soon as she asked the question, she wondered why she'd bothered. She knew the answer.

Nonetheless, Mary Grace provided it. "He wants to boss me."

Leah felt there was probably truth in this perception. She sensed that Mark might be a strict parent—more strict than she was. "Well, if I marry him, we'll probably have to let him make some of the rules. But as of now," she said, "he and I have no plans to live together or marry each other." Was this an honest answer? She tried to be honest with Mary Grace, always honest. "Still," she said, "I'm not going to promise you that it won't happen."

"What if I don't want you to?"

"I'll certainly listen to you, but I'll make the decision for myself. I always try to do what's best for both of us, and Mark might be the best thing for both of us." More and more, she was beginning to suspect this was the case. Not the easiest thing, but the best.

But she knew Mary Grace was right; Mark Logan would want to make the rules. Possibly lots of rules. Leah suspected the two of them could look forward to many battles of will.

Mary Grace said, "I don't like Mark."

"Thank you, Mary Grace, but I expect you to be respectful to him anyhow, just as you would be to anyone."

Mary Grace neither consented to this nor argued with it.

"I CAN'T sleep."

Mark and Leah had played music, Mary Grace sitting with them and happily singing along, for an hour after dinner. Now, having got Mary Grace to bed, Leah sat down on the couch in the living room with Mark, where they planned to look through the gift he'd brought her—a book of names. It had touched her, and she couldn't understand why she felt it so deeply. But now Mary Grace had come out of her room for the third time.

Leah wearily rose from the couch and was struck by the too-familiar pain caused by pressure on her sciatic nerve. Her rear end and her hip area suddenly pulsed with the excruciating pain, and she grabbed the edge of the couch.

Mark was on his feet, beside her, ready to help. "What is it?"

"Sciatica. It's no big deal. Mary Grace, please get back in bed. You can have your light on and look at books if you want."

"I want to be out here."

"Did you hear your mother?"

Leah tried to move, and the pain was incapacitating. She breathed deeply, focusing on her breath as she made herself straighten up.

"You're not in charge," Mary Grace told Mark.

"Mary Grace," Leah repeated, "please go back to your room."

"I need you to tuck me in again."

"I will in a moment."

"Okay." Mary Grace turned and went back into her bedroom.

Mark told Leah, "You're the one who's probably ready for some sleep."

"I'm fine." She made her ungainly way toward her daughter's bedroom, where she hugged and kissed Mary Grace and her stuffed animals again, then said, "Good night, good girl."

Mary Grace said, "Good night," and opened one of her Dr. Seuss books to "read" to her stuffed animals.

As Leah shut the door of Mary Grace's room behind her, Mark stood again, stood as a man who'd been raised to stand when a woman entered a room. He didn't sit again until she settled on the couch.

Mary Grace's door opened again. "Mom? Could you come here?"

"What is it?" Leah asked without getting up.

"Will you check under my bed?"

Mark said, "Your mom's uncomfortable. Let's let her sit down, and I'll check under the bed."

"I want my mom to do it."

Leah started to rise, but Mark was already standing.

"She's sitting down," he repeated.

Leah made herself stand, and he said, "Leah."

"I'm fine."

"That's not the point."

"What isn't?"

"Your job isn't to be at her beck and call."

How dare he propose to tell her what being a mother meant? "Making sure that Mary Grace feels safe and happy certainly *is* my job," Leah said. And Mary Grace, who had never encountered a snake not contained behind glass, had a fear of snakes under the bed.

Mark followed her to Mary Grace's bedroom and watched the little girl in pink pajamas climb into her bed in a room full of stuffed animals and dolls, paints and children's furniture, a room with everything. He watched Leah, whose baby was due in less than two months, get down on hands and knees and peer beneath her daughter's bed.

Torn between appreciation of the kind of mother she was and concern for her, Mark watched Leah. Her hair was in a long braid down her back. He wanted to sit and brush that hair, brush and brush it for hours. He wanted to draw a bath for her, complete with soothing scents and candlelight for relaxation.

He wanted, he knew, to do much more.

"Nothing there," Leah told her daughter. "Good night, now."

"Good night," Mary Grace said.

"And don't get up again," Mark told the four-year-old as Leah stood, "because you're going to have to tuck yourself back in."

Leah frowned, and he knew she would hold her tongue only till they were out of her daughter's room with the door shut behind them.

But he didn't get even that reprieve.

Leah said, "That's not true. Don't tell her she can't get out of bed."

"I didn't," Mark said. "I just told her—"

"That's not your decision." Leah's sciatic nerve throbbed, sending shooting pains throughout her leg and hip.

Mark stared at her, then said, "Fine." He turned and walked out of the room.

Leah said, "Good night, Mary Grace," and bent to kiss her daughter before leaving the room again, shutting the door behind her.

Mark sat on the couch, paging through the book of names but not, Leah believed, reading a single word.

Leah was annoyed by what he'd said to Mary Grace. This was her house. He wasn't even her boyfriend, and he was trying to lay down the law for her daughter. Not their mutual child, but Mary Grace.

This wasn't what she'd had planned for this evening, this evening when she'd begun to believe that what she both wanted and needed was Mark Logan.

Now, he was quiet, focusing on the book, but not focusing. No, just staring.

He said, "I'm sorry. That wasn't my place."

She silently agreed.

"Leah, I want to take this relationship further. I think you're beautiful. We seem to share many of the same ideals. Telling your daughter what to do was a pretty clumsy way to show how I feel about you."

She lifted her eyes. His, an almost turquoise blue, gazed at her frankly. She felt a pulse fluttering at her throat. *After how he just behaved toward Mary Grace,* she thought, *I can't possibly be considering...* "We have different parenting styles. I think a child who feels secure will take healthy attitudes into adulthood."

"I was thinking about you," he said. "You're pregnant, and she has you getting up and down like a jack-in-the-box."

"You say it as though that's what she's trying to do."

He rubbed his jaw. Took a breath. "I guess I did say it that way. I suppose I wonder if she's doing it to interrupt your time with me."

Leah considered. It wasn't out of the realm of possibility. "Even if she is, I need to treat her as I always do. She needs to feel secure."

Mark felt strangely impressed by Leah's attitude. But he also knew that attitude would be a challenge to live with. He said, "People also turn into confident adults by realizing that they don't always have to be at the center of things."

"She's four years old."

"A good time for a bit of a reality check."

Leah shook her head firmly. Mary Grace was not spoiled. She did not whine for toys in the store. She rarely threw anything resembling a temper tantrum.

"But what I'm really wondering," he said, "is if you're as interested in me as I am in you."

"Yes," she said, finding the reply unclear and inadequate.

Mark glanced at her, saw the color in her cheeks, suffusing her smooth pale skin with dark pink.

He put down the book of baby names and touched Leah's hand. Then he smoothed her dark hair back from her face. With his hand cupping her jaw, he kissed her, then drew back to study her eyes, to try to read the reaction there.

Her dark eyes opened and gazed at him. Then she leaned toward him to kiss him back.

Laguna Beach, California
Camille's journal

Dear Diary,

Tish is going to come and stay with me in Colorado. I've told her about my dad's house, how we have to conserve water because he has to haul it in and all kinds of stuff like that. She says maybe there will be cute guys there. I'm like, Hello, Tish? How can there be cute guys there when there's nothing, nothing, nothing?

I'm bummed because if there are guys they're all going to go for her, for obvious reasons.

James still hasn't called me again, so I guess he does think I'm shallow, whatever that means to him.

Chapter Seven

She did not want Mary Grace to awaken and find her in bed with Mark Logan. And as they sat together on the couch, things seemed to be speeding in that direction.

So she whispered to him, "Mary Grace."

He made a small sound which she took for an inhalation. Or a sigh.

But he said, "Of course." He hesitated, then asked, "Have you had a lover since she's been old enough to—" Apparently at a loss for words, he let the question trail off.

"Not since Sam died," she admitted.

"Ah."

"You?" she asked.

"Me, what?" Then he seemed to understand. "It's been a few years. I can channel that energy into work." He paused. "I think I changed when Camille became a little older and I started realizing boys in her class were interested in her...that way. I wanted to set a good example. Or something like that. Perhaps I want to be a responsible father. Even though she doesn't usually live with me."

Leah nodded slowly.

"Leah." He turned, facing her, his own expression serious. "Leah, I want to marry you. I want us to build a life together, with Mary Grace, with Camille to whatever extent she and her mother will let that happen."

"What if it doesn't work out?" Leah whispered.

"Don't you think that's a matter of choice?"

"Whether or not a relationship works out?" Leah asked, trying to clarify.

"Yes."

Maybe he was right. If both partners believed in staying together, believed that a marriage was indissoluble, believed it impossible that it would not endure, maybe the decision to remain married no matter what would keep them together.

Leah wanted to be persuaded, but something held her back.

"Don't you remember how hard marriage is?" she asked Mark.

"I remember that I liked it," he said.

"But don't you remember how angry you could get with Sabrina? I'm sure you must have felt angry with her."

"Oh, yes," he agreed. "But it was more like a puzzle to be figured out for me. It wasn't like…war."

Leah laughed ruefully. Yet again and again it occurred to her that she genuinely *liked* Mark. He'd painted her house and been pleasant to have around while he was doing it. And she'd seen some good interaction between him and Mary Grace. Mary Grace had found the shell of a robin's egg and taken it to show him

The Harlequin Reader Service — Here's how it works:

Accepting your 2 free books and 2 free mystery gifts (gifts valued at approximately $10.00) places you under no obligation to buy anything. You may keep the books and gifts and return the shipping statement marked "cancel." If you do not cancel, about a month later we'll send you 4 additional books and bill you just $4.24 each in the U.S. or $4.99 each in Canada, plus 25¢ shipping and handling per book and applicable taxes if any.* That's the complete price and — at a savings of at least 15% off the cover price — it's quite a bargain! You may cancel at any time, but if you choose to continue, every month we'll send you 4 more books, which you may either purchase at the discount price or return to us and cancel your subscription.

If offer card is missing write to: Harlequin Reader Service, 3010 Walden Ave., P.O. Box 1867, Buffalo NY 14240-1867

BUSINESS REPLY MAIL

FIRST-CLASS MAIL   PERMIT NO. 717   BUFFALO, NY

POSTAGE WILL BE PAID BY ADDRESSEE

HARLEQUIN READER SERVICE
3010 WALDEN AVE
PO BOX 1867
BUFFALO NY 14240-9952

NO POSTAGE
NECESSARY
IF MAILED
IN THE
UNITED STATES

Get FREE BOOKS and
FREE GIFTS when you play the...

LAS VEGAS
GAME

*Just scratch off
the gold box with a coin.
Then check below to see
the gifts you get!*

YES! I have scratched off the gold box. Please send me my **2 FREE BOOKS** and **2 FREE GIFTS** for which I qualify. I understand that I am under no obligation to purchase any books as explained on the back of this card.

354 HDL ESRE   154 HDL ESUQ

FIRST NAME	LAST NAME

ADDRESS

APT.#	CITY

STATE/PROV.	ZIP/POSTAL CODE

(H-AR-11/08)

7	7	7	Worth TWO FREE BOOKS plus TWO FREE GIFTS!
🍒	🍒	🍒	Worth TWO FREE BOOKS!
🔔	🔔	♣	TRY AGAIN!

www.eHarlequin.com

Offer limited to one per household and not va
to current subscribers of Harlequin American
Romance® books. All orders subject to approv

Your Privacy - Harlequin Books is committed to protecting your privacy. Our privacy policy is available online at
www.eHarlequin.com or upon request from the Harlequin Reader Service. From time to time we make our lists
of customers available to reputable third parties who may have a product or service of interest to you. If you
would prefer for us not to share your name and address, please check here. ☐

and he'd told her it was a jewel, and she'd liked that. So had Leah. And tonight, bringing the book of names. He'd asked her casually if she'd thought about names. A little, she'd admitted, but she wanted to think on it some more and hear his thoughts. So he'd brought the book.

Was she in love with him? Leah had become such a pragmatist that she almost didn't consider the question as a large part of the equation. Because she believed in the idea that you could *learn* to love. She was attracted to him; that part could not be learned. And she believed he was good, that he was a good man.

She said softly, "It's crazy to think about marrying now."

"Why?"

"Because we don't know each other." And yet they did. Mark was River's brother. They'd known each other for years. But Leah had always maintained that she didn't like him. *Perhaps because when I first met him Sam was alive and we were married?* Now, a part of her admitted that she'd always found him attractive—and perhaps found reasons to dislike him because of it.

"I think," he said, "we do know each other, Leah."

But Mary Grace...

"Mark, I'm always going to do what I think is best for Mary Grace. I'm not sure you really understand that."

His smile was quiet and oddly self-deprecating. "I doubt I'd want to marry you if I thought otherwise."

Leah blinked. "You won't fight me at every corner?"

"I hope we can make some decisions together, Leah."

Of course. "All right, then," she said. "Okay."

"Okay, what?"

"I will marry you."

A smile split his face, and she realized that she'd never seen him smile like this. He said after a moment, "I suppose I have some work to do to get Mary Grace to like me."

"Her only complaint seems to be that you're bossy."

"She's not the first person to say it."

Leah laughed, liking him for the answer. She sat on the couch with him for another half hour, then went to Mary Grace's door. Her daughter had fallen asleep with her light on, books spread over the entire surface of her bed. Leah went in, moved the books back to their shelves and pulled the cover up under Mary Grace's chin.

Then she turned out the light, stepped out into the hall and closed her daughter's door.

Mark stood at the kitchen sink, washing up the last of the dinner dishes.

"That halo looks good on you," Leah told him.

He laughed.

Fifteen minutes later, he turned out the lights in the living room on the way to Leah's bedroom.

She slept on a double-bed-size futon on a plain frame. Seeing it, Mark reflected that he should buy the two of them a new bed for a wedding present; he was six foot four.

He sat on the bed beside Leah and kissed her again.

She trembled slightly, and he said, "Is everything all right?"

"Yes. Yes. Fine."

"We don't have to do this now," he said, though he thought he might choke on the words. He would prefer slitting his own throat to not finally making love with Leah as he wanted.

"It's not that," she said.

He decided that if she had something to tell him, she would. He reached for the lamp on the bedside table and turned it out.

MARK LEFT Mary Grace and Leah at the Delta Children's Museum on Saturday afternoon and drove on alone to the Montrose airport. Camille would be arriving by herself. Her friend Tish would fly in the following weekend.

Leah had urged Mark to take his time coming back for them, letting Camille start to adjust to the news. As Leah and Mary Grace stopped at the dinosaur exhibit to make a plaster-of-Paris footprint track, the four-year-old asked for the third time, "Will I meet my new sister today?"

"Probably," Leah said. "But she probably won't be ready to think of you as a sister yet." Her daughter's displeasure at learning that her mother intended to marry Mark Logan had been tempered by the prospect of having a big sister. "You know how there are some things you don't like about Mark?"

"Yes."

"Well, Camille might have some of those feelings toward you and me."

"But we're nice!" Mary Grace exclaimed.

Leah laughed. "I think Mark's pretty nice, too."

"He's okay," Mary Grace said, showing the adaptability Leah so admired in her.

Mark had told Camille that he had a new job in Paonia so that they'd be living there. He and Leah both wanted them all to live together, and he thought that Camille might prefer Leah's offer that her office become Camille's bedroom to the extreme rusticity of the Wilderness Challenge "base house." Mark also had some concerns about Camille being so near the office twenty-four hours a day. He liked the kids he'd met on the job, but that didn't mean he wanted his daughter to go out with recent gang members, meth addicts and the like.

Leah smiled a little as she remembered him saying, "With my luck, Camille will decide she can't live without one of these guys." Leah agreed it sounded like an explosive combination.

Camille, he reported, had asked, "So what's the population of Paonia? Three?"

But the thought of living in a place with a more abundant supply of hot water, not to mention reliable cell-phone reception and high-speed Internet service had seemed like an improvement, as far as Camille was concerned.

So Leah tried to focus on enjoying the afternoon with Mary Grace, instead of worrying about how the two of them—and the news of the baby—would be received by Camille.

MARK SAW the commuter plane from Denver taxi past the window. He felt slightly ill. *Should* he have told her over the phone? Leah had urged him to. Now, he wished he'd taken her advice.

The problem was, he'd been afraid. Not of her anger, though she might well be angry. More of her emotions—and of what coping mechanisms she might use. It made him feel minimally safer to know that he could see her face when he dealt her this blow. It made him believe that *she* would be safer, less likely to do some out-of-control teenage thing.

Then, Camille was there, coming through the glass doors, past security and out into the airport, and Mark's heart rushed with love for her and pride in her. She was very blond and not just pretty but beautiful, tall and slim as a model, her hair sweeping round her shoulders over the small gold hoops sparkling on the lobes of her tiny ears. She saw him and hurried toward him, a purse slung over her shoulder, even as she drew out her cell phone and switched it on to check for messages.

Seeing the gesture, he laughed.

Almost absently, she hugged her father. "Hi, Dad. I told Tish we'd pick her up next week. We will, won't we?"

"Of course. Your bags are checked?"

Camille nodded, looking toward the baggage claim. "Is there coffee here? Like, Starbucks?"

"In Montrose. And there's a local place in Paonia." Camille loved cappuccinos. "Did you get lunch on the plane? Or shall we get something?"

"I could do with a salad."

"I know just the place." They stood awkwardly waiting for Camille's bags, then he said, "I have some news. I don't know quite how to tell you."

"You're getting married," she said in the flat and blithe voice of someone who believes her father will never remarry. She was making a joke.

"Yes. That's part of it."

Her head spun. "I was just kidding!"

"I hope you'll like her," Mark said. "She's a midwife. She has a four-year-old daughter. And—she and I are having a baby."

"Oh," Camille said in a tone both bright and deliberately snotty, a voice she'd been using since the sixth grade. "Surprise."

Mark glanced uneasily at his daughter. He felt the usual mixture of feelings seeing her after months apart. Pride that she was related to him. Pleasure at seeing her again. Horror at how mature and sophisticated she looked. And, most of all, terror. Terror that somehow he wouldn't measure up. That she would hate him and reject him and everything he stood for. Plus determination not to be other than who he was. "Leah wanted me to tell you over the phone." He drew a deep breath and made himself say, "The pregnancy came about in—an unusual way."

She lifted her eyebrows, and he could see distaste at the prospect of hearing any details of conception warring with reluctant curiosity.

"River and Leah's sister, Ellen, asked us to be surrogate parents."

"Oh, my God, she's Aunt Ellen's sister!"

"What's wrong with that?"

Camille's expression eloquently conveyed insults she wouldn't risk saying out loud. With apparent restraint, she said, "Nothing, except that she's a New Age air-head."

"Leah isn't," Mark said. "And I'm not agreeing that your aunt is."

"You mean, you're having a baby for her to keep? You're not keeping it," Camille clarified, darting looks between the luggage carousel and the screen of her cell phone.

"We are keeping it, Camille."

"She was your girlfriend, and you planned to have a baby for her sister—"

"No. This was all done in the impersonal way such things are usually managed."

"Now I've heard everything," his daughter murmured, shaking her head.

"But then your aunt and uncle got pregnant, too, and Leah and I— Well, we get on."

"You've known her, like, a few months, and you're going to marry her." Camille stated this as fact, her disgust apparent in her tone of voice.

"No, I've known her for years. As I said, she's Ellen's sister."

"And this is why you moved to Paonia," Camille continued, surmising the truth.

Mark drew his answer out with his next breath. "Y-yes."

"And I have a ready-made little sister I'll no doubt be expected to babysit, so that you two can have some time together?"

Mark stared at her, astonished that she would expect such a thing from him. But why not? He'd already done two things she hadn't anticipated. "Of course not. We're not thinking of you as a ready-made babysitter."

Camille cast a look at him. "But we'll be living with them."

"Yes. You'll have your own room. Leah is letting you use her midwifery office."

"Gee, thanks," said Camille without enthusiasm.

He said, "You and I will go camping, as usual, and—"

"Is that supposed to be a favor?"

"No. It's supposed to be spending time together. I'm your dad. I like to spend time with you. And you usually have a good time."

She suddenly strode away, toward the luggage wheel.

Mark saw the familiar suitcase with wheels. Prada. Sabrina had bought Camille Prada luggage the year before. He'd had no idea what the set must have cost until one of his employees had enlightened him. He truly didn't understand. He didn't see why anyone would spend that much money on luggage, let alone why his ex-wife should spend so much on a set for a teenager who traveled twice a year.

Mark's strides reached Camille's first bag before his daughter could touch it. He lifted it from the luggage carousel and set it down.

Camille said, "So, when's the test-tube baby coming?"

"The baby wasn't conceived in vitro."

Camille said, "Whatever."

"The due date is July thirty-first."

"Are you getting married before or after? There's

the other one." She nodded at a suitcase emerging into the carousel.

He collected the bag before answering her. "We haven't decided. But we'd like you to be there."

"When the baby's born?" Camille managed to look as though she found the suggestion to be in the worst possible taste.

"I meant for the wedding," Mark said. "But you might still be in Colorado when the baby comes."

"I can't wait."

Mark placed her bags onto a cart, and Camille trailed after him as they left the airport terminal. Before they reached his parking space, Camille was on her phone, listening to messages.

When they were both in the car, Mark asked, "Food first? Or coffee?"

"I'm not hungry," she answered coldly.

LEAH had expected Camille Logan to be pretty but wasn't prepared for how sophisticated she looked, nor how the scent of money exuded from her. When Mark introduced them outside the library—Leah had left him a message that she and Mary Grace would go there after the museum—Camille managed a rather strained smile. "It's nice to meet you," she said.

She was tall, and her high-heeled sandals made her only a few inches shorter than her father.

Leah said, "And you." Aware of Mary Grace beside her, surprisingly solemn and clinging to the fabric of her maternity dress, she added, "We have some things for you."

Silently, Mary Grace presented a picture that she had drawn at the children's museum. Mary Grace had used the tools provided at the museum—stencils, different textured surfaces to put the paper on before shading—to create something rather special.

Camille's face softened slightly as she took the picture. "Thank you," she said, looking down at Mary Grace.

"It's a princess and a bear," Mary Grace said.

"I like it," Camille said.

"And this is from me." Leah handed Camille a small gift-wrapped box. She had purchased the gift the day before in Paonia, from the local artists' gallery. Now, she waited uneasily. Camille's style was rather classic; her gift might be too funky for her.

"Thank you," Camille said. She hesitated a moment, then unwrapped the tiny box, opened it and peeled back the dark-pink tissue paper.

Handmade earrings of fired metals, links of graduating sizes and different shapes—octagons, triangles, circles and so on.

"Wow," Camille said. "I like these."

Leah breathed a sigh of relief. "A woman in Paonia makes them. I didn't know your style…" She let her sentence drift off.

But Camille was taking out her gold hoops and putting on the new earrings.

"Let's see," said Mark, craning his head around to see her face. "They look good on you."

"I want a mirror," Camille said and opened her purse.

"There's one in the truck," Mark told her. "Let's get home. If everyone's ready?"

Leah nodded. Mary Grace had let go of her dress and was now gazing up at Camille as though mesmerized.

Leah instinctively liked Mark's daughter. She sensed both vulnerability and curiosity in the girl, neither far from the surface. She seemed bemused by Mary Grace, as someone who hadn't spent much time around children and wasn't sure what to expect.

Mark opened the back door of his vehicle for her, and Camille murmured, "Thanks," sounding slightly ironic. She had her cell phone out and was punching a code in.

Mary Grace's car seat was on the other side of the backseat, and Leah belted her daughter in. Mary Grace watched Camille solemnly. Leah knew the child sensed the nervousness between Camille and herself, all the awkwardness of the meeting. Leah asked her, "Would you like your Barbie?"

Mary Grace reached beside her seat, trying to find the Barbie doll she'd brought. Leah handed it to her along with a small box containing doll clothes and accessories.

Mark drove while Leah checked her cell phone for messages. It had been on the whole time, set to vibrate rather than ring. There were no messages. She hadn't heard from her sister since telling her the time of her appointment with Dr. Holmes. She'd asked Ellen to call her if the bleeding resumed. Leah debated calling her sister then gave in to the impulse, seeing as Camille was holding her own long-distance conversation.

"Hi, it's me," the teenager said in the backseat. "I'm here. Oh, it's real interesting here, believe me…"

River answered, and Leah identified herself.

"Hey, Leah. Ellen's not here."

"Where is she?" *I told her to rest.*

"Just wanted to go into town. Went to the store. Can I give her a message?"

"I asked her to rest, River."

"You know Ellen. She says it doesn't feel right to rest."

Tension tightened Leah's chest. "Has the bleeding stopped?"

"Yes, actually. She wouldn't have gone if it hadn't. Actually, she seems better than she has yet during the pregnancy."

River, like Mark, could sometimes inspire great confidence. Leah felt herself relax. "That's terrific news. But please encourage her to take it easy."

"Ah. You'll be pleased to know that I persuaded her to let me prune the rosebushes."

"Oh, what a relief. Thank you," Leah said.

"And she's going to go to the doctor. She doesn't want an ultrasound, though. Do you think it's twins?"

"It's too soon to detect with a fetoscope. The fundus is measuring large for age, though. Danine said she had a vision or something—or could feel two souls. That's how the whole question came up. But it's not impossible that Ellen is carrying twins."

"That sounds like Danine," River said.

Leah remembered with gratitude what a steadying influence River was in Ellen's life. He was a realist.

Leah ended the call feeling better. She'd had difficult clients in the past, but never had she referred anyone to another practitioner for personality reasons. Yet lately she'd wondered if she would really be the best care provider for Ellen. Well, after the appointment with Dr. Holmes, they'd all know more.

Their parents had been gone for five years now, one dying swiftly after the other. Leah and Ellen had grown up in Denver. They'd always been opposites, Leah the responsible older sibling and Ellen the carefree younger. But they'd always lived near each other, always remained friends. Leah had watched her sister make many impulsive decisions. Ellen was flighty, had changed religions four times in her adult life, always with fanaticism. But her marriage to River had seemed to change Ellen for the better. She'd become steadier, taking her steadiness from the veteran who operated each day and each year by the rising and setting of the sun, moving at nature's pace, working as an organic farmer for the peace it brought him. That peace had rubbed off on Ellen.

But Ellen could still be a little wild.

Leah had dealt with other clients—many other clients—with extreme belief systems. Vegans who would never eat any produce not organically grown. People who followed regimented macrobiotic diets or who lived according to strict Ayurvedic principles. Or the raw-food contingent. Or the woman who must, must, *must* give birth to her child in the water.

She'd been able to deal with some very difficult personalities in the midwife-client relationship. None of them had set her off balance the way Ellen had, because of the emotions involved.

She heard Camille, in the backseat, beginning another phone conversation. "Hi, it's me. Yeah, I'm here. Paonia. I've never been there. I think it's full of hippies.... Actually, I don't think of him that way, but maybe you're right...."

Her father, Leah decided. Someone had probably suggested that Mark was a hippie. Leah had certainly never thought of him that way.

"She *did?* Is she going to do it?"

Mark and Leah exchanged the briefest of glances. They had reached the traffic light at Olathe, north of Montrose.

"Would *you* do it?" Camille asked.

Leah found herself curious what someone Camille knew had done.

"Well," Camille said, "let's say it's already full of surprises."

Her trip to Colorado—the surprises being Leah, Mary Grace and the pregnancy.

When Camille ended this conversation, Mark said, "I wondered if you might want to earn some money helping me at the Wilderness Challenge office this summer." He'd thought this through. He would know the days when their teenage clients would be out in the wilderness; on those days, Camille could come to the office and help with logistics. There were tents and other equipment to be sorted, and Jason had agreed that Mark could hire his daughter to help in the supply warehouse and the office.

"I'll help!" Mary Grace said.

He smiled, the real smile which Leah had seen for the first time the night she'd agreed to marry him, the night they'd become lovers.

"Thank you," Mark told Mary Grace. "I'm sure I can find work for you."

"Are you going to work in the mountains at all?" Camille asked, sounding almost wistful.

"About once a week. You can come up there with me."

"Are you going to sell the business?"

The hut system, his guide service. "If I get a fair offer. But we'll keep the house on the Dallas Divide."

"But you'll live down here," Camille concluded.

"Yes." Mark glanced once in the rearview mirror, perhaps gauging his daughter's reaction.

Leah said, "Also, I saw one of the river outfits is looking for office help. The river guides are cute."

Mark's eyes went wide, and he said, "But *old*. And Camille doesn't want to spend her whole summer working."

"How old?" Camille asked. Leah, glancing into the backseat, saw that Camille was assessing her, perhaps wondering if they had the same definition of *cute*.

"Thirty-five," Mark said.

Camille made a face.

Leah said, "Some of them are college students."

"Thirty-five-year-old college students," Camille said. "Better late than never, I guess."

Leah laughed. "I *meant* that some of them are in their late teens and early twenties. *More* than are thirty-five." She changed the subject, asking Camille, "Where do you want to go to school?"

"Pepperdine," Camille said matter-of-factly. "But it's not that easy to get in. My stepfather's an alumnus, though."

"Do you know what you want to do?" Leah asked.

Camille shrugged. "Maybe be a personal trainer. I

like to work out. But I'm not really an athlete. I've done some modeling."

"You have?" Mark said. Why hadn't she told him this?

"I did a bridal fashion show in April at the Galleria," she said. "But my options there are a bit limited by nature."

There was a cold edge to her words, and Leah guessed the subject of breast implants was being raised for the first time.

"I'll be able to get more jobs in September," she said.

Mark gathered from this that she planned to have the surgery in August. Impotent, he drove on, trying to think what to say, managing, "So—what about doing some work for me?"

"I don't need the money," she said.

Again, he tried to tamp down his anger, to wish it away, to wish the world different. He would not have raised her like this.

But he hadn't raised her, so his anger was with himself for agreements made when she was small. And with a judge who'd believed children needed much more time with mothers than fathers. He'd had a good idea of the life Sabrina would provide for her.

"In that case," he made himself say, "how about some river trips?" The Wilderness Challenge office was near the river, and river-rafting was part of the curriculum. Mark owned a boat of his own. Once again, he could keep Camille separate from the clients. "You could go with me or with Leah and Mary Grace." There was one section of the river which was safe for a pregnant woman and a four-year-old—with life vests, of course.

Camille shrugged. "Whatever."

Paonia, Colorado
Camille's journal

Dear Diary,

I so cannot believe what it's like here. I can't believe my dad expects me to spend the summer with him and his pregnant girlfriend and her little kid. The closest shopping is Grand Junction, which, believe me, is not shopping. Leah said something about driving me to Breckenridge for shopping. She said there are stores she thinks I'd like.

I can tell shopping's not really her thing.

Anyhow, I go to work with Dad sometimes, and, yeah, I've seen some cute river guides down at the put-in, but they didn't look twice at me. There's a river outfit just a short way from the Wilderness Challenge office. Wilderness Challenge is for delinquents, and I haven't seen any, since Dad doesn't want me working on days when they're around. He hasn't *said* so, but I'm sure that's what he's thinking. There's a hot-springs pool here, like in Ouray, and I've been going there, and there are some cute guys.

I wanted Tish to come, but it's going to be really depressing if the guys all like her. I want to learn to kayak. This guide Deke who's really old and works for Wilderness Challenge says there's a "learning curve" with kayaking. My dad says that means it's hard to learn. Anyhow, Dad is willing to teach me, and so is Deke. Leah knows how to kayak, too, but she said she hasn't been for years, since her first husband was alive.

Leah is very beautiful. She reminds me of the woman in *Last of the Mohicans,* I forget her name. I don't want to babysit her kid. The one that's walking around or the new one.

Chapter Eight

"You're moving to Cannes," Mark repeated into his cell phone. Sabrina was on the other end. The news pulled at him in different ways. His ex-wife and her husband were moving to France—for a year. It would be good for Camille to live in Europe, he thought, good for her to get a chance to improve her high-school French. On the other hand, she'd be farther away. The ticket back at Christmas would be more expensive. He could manage that; it was just the distance, the separation.

Camille had been with them for two weeks; her friend Tish had been with them for one. The two girls seemed to be having fun, though Camille seemed moody and dissatisfied. Leah said Camille was obsessed with body image, but Mark thought his daughter was much too pretty for her own good and couldn't imagine how she could be unhappy with any aspect of her appearance. *He* was less than happy that her nose was neither his nor Sabrina's but the recreation of a plastic surgeon, but there was nothing wrong with the way she looked.

"It's all happened very suddenly," Sabrina said on the other line.

Mark stared out the dusty window of the river-outfit office, watching one of the guides check that the rafts were secure on the trailer that would take them to the put-in. It was sweltering outside but cool in the Wilderness Challenge office, which was shaded by cottonwoods and Russian olive trees.

Jason was out of the country now, climbing in the Alps. Mark had implemented some new safety protocols in Jason's absence, letting him know of the changes via e-mail and receiving Jason's lackadaisical okay. Mark believed that everyone at Wilderness Challenge, workers and clients alike, might fare better if the business became a nonprofit, but Jason said that he wanted to "build it up" and "sell it." Mark was already looking for additional work in the off-season, to increase his income then.

"So we're going at the end of July," Sabrina said. "We've rented the house in the interim."

"When will Camille join you?" he asked, hopeful, as always, that it would be convenient for Sabrina if their daughter spent a longer visit with him.

"Oh, I thought I said. That's why I called. I thought she'd live with you this year. And we're— well, things are going to be hectic there. He's got so much industry business. And we're not sure it's a good environment for a teenager. Besides, it will keep her away from the divorce."

Mark had never heard Sabrina suggest that anywhere on earth wouldn't be a good environment for Camille.

One word, however, seemed to explain. "What divorce?"

"Oh, well—Camille doesn't know yet. Glenn and I— Well, we're going our separate ways."

His mind spun. Camille and Tish were down at the river, getting kayaking lessons from Deke. It was Camille's second lesson, Tish's first, and he had a feeling Tish was going to hate rolling, hate getting her hair wet. Whereas Camille was a bit like a terrier with something between her teeth, *determined* to learn and be good at kayaking, probably to impress Jared, the Wilderness Challenge guide who Camille said looked like a *GQ* model.

Camille did not know her mother and stepfather were getting a divorce. She called Glenn "Glenn," but the man had been part of her life for more than a decade.

"I thought you'd be glad to have Camille with you," she said.

"I am," he agreed. *But Camille's not going to be thrilled.* Moving to Paonia, Colorado, in her junior year of high school. "How were you planning to get her belongings out here?"

"Oh, we'll ship them. I already have Alma packing them."

The servant.

"And when are you going to break the news to Camille?" he said.

"Don't you want to?"

"I don't think it's my place to tell her that you and Glenn are getting a divorce."

"I don't object," she said.

"Well, I do," he told her. "One or preferably both of you should tell her."

"Well, I can't drop everything and fly out to Colorado. We have too much to do here, Mark. I suppose I can call her and tell her—or Glenn can."

"Good idea," he said, gritting his teeth. "By the way, if you're not going to Cannes with Glenn, who is *we?*"

"My fiancé. Richard. He's a director."

Mark tried to work through the concept of simultaneously having a fiancé and a spouse. He settled for saying, "I am very happy to have Camille living with me, but I'm sorry for the pain she's going to suffer over this."

"It's not like he's her real dad," Sabrina said airily. "You are."

Mark thought Sabrina was dramatically underestimating the importance of Glenn in Camille's life, so he said nothing. Just began wondering if Leah knew any counselors in the area who would be good talking with frustrated sixteen-year-old girls.

Because he was pretty sure that was what he'd soon have on his hands.

Among other things, Camille was desperately anticipating breast-augmentation surgery in August. And he wasn't about to give his consent.

MARK WONDERED whether Tish's presence would make news of the divorce easier or harder for Camille. After some time he'd gotten a promise from Sabrina that, if the news was not to be given to Camille to her face, it should be given soon.

He was still at the office that evening when Glenn called.

Mark had long since put aside most of his bitterness at Sabrina's infidelity with Glenn during her marriage to Mark. Glenn was Camille's stepfather, and Mark had found over the years that he preferred Glenn's parenting style to Sabrina's.

Glenn said, "Sabrina told me about your conversation with her. I'm of the opinion that Camille needs the chance to talk with us about this in person. Sabrina may not be willing, but I am. How would you feel if I came out to Colorado and spent some time with her, let her know that I still plan to be part of her life?"

Mark considered briefly, then found he was grateful. "Wonderful idea."

"I'm sure you've got a full house. Can you recommend a good hotel? Also, I think it would be best if I told her over the phone, then came out."

Mark thought briefly, then saw the wisdom in the plan. In any event, he couldn't dictate how Sabrina and Glenn told Camille about the divorce. When he'd ended the call, he shut the door of the back office and phoned Leah.

CAMILLE WAS on her cell phone, Tish hanging next to her, trying to hear. "Camp starts August third?" Camille said. "No, I'll be back by then. Thanks, Samantha!"

She ended the call, and then both girls began jumping up and down, screaming.

Leah, cutting vegetables for a salad in the kitchen while Mary Grace played with her Barbie dolls on the living-room floor, watched the two teenagers hugging each other. She couldn't help smiling. Over the past few days, she'd really come to enjoy having teenage girls in the house. They were silly about some things but also strangely ambitious in unusual ways. Tish wanted to be an actress. She had modeled in the same bridal fashion show that Camille had. And Camille sometimes joined in singing when Mark and Leah played music together in the evening. She had a very pretty alto. Tish sang sometimes, too, very softly, as though unsure of herself.

Leah knew that Tish had breast implants because Camille had mentioned it, and Leah had to admit that Tish's body looked a bit unnatural. She was lanky like Camille, her legs sticklike, and on top of it all was a set of enormous breasts. Tish herself had told Leah that she got regular Botox injections to ward off future wrinkles. Like Camille, she'd had her nose done, and the two noses were remarkably similar.

Now, the two girls jumping up and down and screaming in her living room looked almost like sisters.

Mary Grace, eyebrows drawn together in annoyance, moved her dolls out of danger of jumping teenage feet.

Walking gingerly, always wary of the next attack of sciatica, Leah entered the living room and gripped the back of one of the chairs. "It sounds like you got good news."

"I made the cheerleading squad!" Camille shouted.

Leah's heart sank. Mark had phoned her three times that day about Sabrina's divorce and move to France. Now, it was 8:00 p.m., and he still wasn't home, and she knew it was because he dreaded seeing his daughter and having to pretend, having to keep from her the knowledge that her mother and stepfather had yet to impart to the girl.

Now, Camille had made cheerleader, and she was ecstatic, unaware that she'd be spending the coming school year not in California but in Colorado.

"I mean, the other girl, the girl I almost beat at tryouts, she's moving, so I got her place!"

Tish and Camille shrieked again.

Tish said, "This is so great. I can start teaching you the routines."

What a mess, Leah thought. She knew the anguish Camille was going to suffer when she learned of the divorce, let alone the move to Colorado.

She felt desperate for Camille to know the facts, to start adjusting. *And I'm engaged and have a baby coming and a new family to manage.* Now, the family was going to include Camille, not as a summer and Christmas visitor but as someone with them all the time.

Her own cell phone rang and she went to pick it up. Ellen.

Leah tensed. Ellen had been to her first appointment with Dr. Holmes and had called Leah right afterward. She was carrying twins, and Ellen was amazed by Danine's "gift," that she had *known.* Then, she'd complained because the physician had called her pregnancy "high-risk." Leah explained that Dr. Holmes would have termed any pregnancy with multiple fetuses high-risk, but Ellen had said, "That's just it. I'm perfectly healthy."

Leah had pointed out that her sister had experienced bleeding. Towards the end of their last conversation, Leah had exclaimed, "Don't you care if those babies survive, Ellen?"

It had been unforgivable. She'd apologized immediately for saying it, but the fact that the words had come out of her mouth reinforced her feeling that she should have as little as possible to do with her sister's pregnancy, labor and birth.

Now she said, "Hello?"

"Hi," said Ellen in a sulky voice.

"How are you?" Leah made herself ask her sister.

"Oh, all right, for someone who can look forward to a hospital birth, hooked up to every machine known to man."

"Is that what Dr. Holmes said?"

"It's what I know."

"You might want to try to visualize it differently," Leah said. She made herself look forward to when her little sister would be the mother of twins—identical twin boys, according to the ultrasound. "Have you and River talked about names?"

"Not really. I mean I've thought about it."

And about the reality of caring for two babies instead of just one? Neither Leah nor the elderly Dr. Holmes had absolutely ruled out a birth outside of the hospital for Ellen. But Leah didn't feel comfortable with the labor taking place so far from the hospital, and neither did her backup physician, who had himself been born at home in Montrose, Colorado, decades before.

Dr. Holmes had noticed Leah's unusual tension in dealing with Ellen. However, he seemed far more comfortable with that than with Leah's earlier decision to have a child for her sister and River. His most recent words to Leah about Ellen's pregnancy had been, "Don't worry. She'll settle down as the time gets nearer."

Leah doubted that. She knew that he meant that as the time for the birth drew nearer Ellen would feel the gravity of her situation.

Leah said, "Hey, I found a breast pump for you. A client whose birth I attended in Carbondale."

"I won't use an electric pump," Ellen said. "It's not like I have to go to work or anything."

"Okay, well, I'm giving you this one anyhow," Leah told her. "You certainly don't have to use it."

"Especially on cloudy days," Ellen said coldly. Their house relied on solar power and one very small, unreliable generator.

Leah remembered one winter when Sam had practically had fits laughing about Ellen and River walking around with headlamps on every night. The memory made her smile. Leah made herself say, "I'm excited for you." It occurred to her that maybe Ellen was depressed. She'd seen postpartum depression, but she'd never seen a first-time mother who had longed for a child depressed during pregnancy. She might mention it to Dr. Holmes.

"I guess I'm excited, too," Ellen said. "It's just that none of it's happening the way I thought it would. I'm not bleeding, so at least I don't have to be in bed, but everyone keeps telling me not to do too much."

Leah felt sympathy with this complaint. She would hate it, too.

While she was talking with her sister, Camille's cell phone rang again. Leah watched Mark's daughter look at the screen. "It's Glenn," she told Tish, and answered the call.

Leah listened to Ellen talking about bindweed in her garden, thinking that she and her sister both shared that, a love of gardening. But she was also watching Camille, watching her face as she said, "Hi, Glenn. Guess what? You know how I didn't make the cheerleading squad? Well, one of the girls can't do it, and I was the runner-up. So I'm in!"

Leah pitied Glenn, knowing the man was about to break Camille's heart. "Ellen, I've got to go. I have to call Mark." Because he needed to come home and be there for Camille.

"What? Sure," Camille was saying.

Mark answered his phone. "I'm just leaving," he told Leah. "I'll be home in ten minutes."

"Good. Well, Camille just got some exciting news which I'm sure she'll tell you herself. Her stepfather just called. She's talking to him now." *So get back here, damn it!*

"I hear you," Mark said. "See you soon."

Leah sat down on the floor with Mary Grace and picked up one of the Barbie dolls. "Can I change her clothes?"

"Yes," Mary Grace said. "She's wearing that—" a navy-blue skirt and blazer "—because she's going to work now."

Undressing the doll to change her clothes, Leah kept one eye on Camille, watching the gradual change in her face.

Camille said, "This can't be true."

Hell! Leah thought. If only it couldn't be true, if only Camille could be safe from the pain of this news, from the shattering of her world.

"Well," the teenager said after a minute, "I can live with you, right?" A brief pause. "Well, I'll tell him I want to live with you! I don't want to move away from Laguna Beach."

More conversation.

"Why?" Camille demanded. "Why can't you stay in Laguna Beach? Mom doesn't need to do that. She doesn't have to sell the house."

Tish had begun to look uneasy. Finally, she sat down on the floor with Mary Grace and Leah and asked if she could play, too.

Camille began to cry. "This isn't fair." She went into her room and shut the door.

Tish looked questioningly at the door, then at Leah. Leah could not enlighten her.

It seemed an eternity before the front door opened and Mark came in. He looked to Leah, and she nodded to Camille's door. He crossed the living room in a few long strides, then paused at Camille's closed door and knocked.

Tish pretended interest in the dolls' plans.

Mary Grace said, "This one looks like you. I'm going to call her Tish."

TISH'S VISIT lasted another week, and Leah felt for the girl as she struggled to cheer up Camille, who was angry, sullen and miserable. Leah knew that Camille's friend would prefer to leave early under the circumstances, but she showed great mettle in attempting to comfort her friend, even going so far as to agree to another kayaking lesson in the hope of making Camille feel better. Leah commented to Mark when the girls set out to walk downtown together, "I'm sorry she's going to be separated from that friend, Mark."

"I'm not," he said firmly. "At least here she won't be surrounded by girls who want a cosmetic surgeon to alter every unique aspect of their looks."

"Tish is a nice girl," Leah replied, "and a good friend to Camille. I like her."

He shrugged. "I like her better than I thought I would. And I'm glad that she's here for Camille to talk to. But inevitably, she's going to go home at some point and Camille will have to get used to a new reality. I don't think it has hit her yet."

"I do," Leah told him. "But I also think she's still hoping that either her mother or Glenn will decide to remain in Laguna Beach for her."

Glenn was due to visit his stepdaughter the day after Tish went home. Meanwhile, Leah was making adjustments in her midwifery practice because of the loss of her office. She now saw clients in the master bedroom, which she kept immaculate for the purpose.

On the day of Glenn's arrival, when Mark, Camille and Mary Grace had gone to the airport to meet his plane, Leah received a phone call from a woman across town.

"Leah, it's Suzanne Keller. I'm not calling for me. Sadie wanted to call you herself." Sadie was Suzanne's daughter, now a junior or senior in high school.

Leah waited but knew.

"She's pregnant, and she wants to have a home birth, and she's planning to keep the baby."

Leah said, "How old is Sadie?"

"Seventeen, just."

"I'd certainly be happy to meet with her," Leah replied.

"I want to come along."

A suffering *"Mom!"* moaned in the background.

Leah knew Sadie Keller as an unusually levelheaded girl with an interest in dance and performance arts. She'd spent summers studying dance in Crested Butte, Denver and Grand Junction. She wore her shoe-polish-black hair in a ragged bob but had no body piercings or tattoos, which made her a bit unusual among her friends.

Sadie was a minor, but if Sadie also planned to keep the baby she would have to grow up fast. Leah understood her mother's protectiveness, would have felt the same way herself, but she also knew that the greater the responsibility Sadie took in her own pregnancy, the better the outcome would be in all ways.

She said, "If Sadie feels more comfortable coming alone, Suzanne, I think it might be a good idea to let her. It's very likely that as her pregnancy progresses, she'll start to rely on you more. But for now maybe let her do this."

"I guess you're right," Suzanne agreed.

A moment later, Sadie herself took the phone from her mother to make her appointment. Sadie explained that she needed to come after three on a weekday. She was working full-time in the office of Paonia's only dentist during the summer and waiting tables at night.

Leah liked the calm sobriety with which Sadie scheduled her first prenatal. She prayed everything would go right for the young woman.

Mark and Mary Grace arrived home without Camille, who had gone for coffee with her stepfather. Glenn had rented a car and would bring her back before dinner. Then, Glenn wanted to take them all out to eat.

Leah had been lying down, when Mark and Mary Grace came back, and while Mary Grace went to her bedroom and began playing, Mark sat on the bed beside Leah, rubbing her legs, trying to lessen the discomfort from her sciatica.

"It will be good for her to have him here," Mark said.

Leah saw from his face, however, that he was worried about Camille. As soon as Tish had left, Camille had fallen into a dark funk, watching television all day, not interested in going outside or anything else. She wasn't unkind to Mary Grace, but she never accepted when the four-year-old asked her to do something with her.

"She should probably talk to a counselor," Leah said. "She probably feels as though none of the adults in her life care about her happiness."

"That's certainly what she says," Mark agreed. He lay down on the bed beside her and put his hand on her stomach, feeling the roundness beneath her spaghetti-strap cotton dress. He felt the baby kick.

"The kid knows you're here," Leah said with a smile.

"What was your labor with Mary Grace like?" Mark asked.

Leah bit her lip. "Twenty-six hours. Not all hard labor, fortunately." She paused. "And Sabrina's with Camille?"

"What I remember most of all was that the cord was around her neck three times and she was blue. But the midwife didn't cut the cord. She unlooped it."

Leah nodded. After a moment, she said, "I think she'll be okay, Mark. Once she starts school and makes friends here."

"She says she wishes she was dead."

"Will she go to a counselor?"

"She might," he said.

"If she will, let's make that happen."

Paonia, Colorado
Camille's journal

Dear Diary,

I can't believe that just when I was about to have everything I want in LB, this has happened. I asked Leah if cheerleading is a big deal here—not that I have the option, tryouts probably have gone by. Leah said she doesn't think so. There's not even a football team. Basketball, soccer, skiing. All the kids I've seen who are my age seem like they're lost, stuck in this nowhere town like I am.

I don't want to do anything. Nothing is going to make it better. Mom said she'd still pay for breast implants, but Dad said if I'm living with him he won't give consent. He and Mom are already sending custody paperwork back and forth. It's like she doesn't care about me. All she cares about is this guy she's met who is going to take her to France. She never would have let Dad have custody of me before this, and now she won't even pay for a lawyer to help me get more of my own rights. Anyhow, Dad says the breast enhancement isn't going to happen.

I'd think Leah would be totally against it, being so natural and a midwife and stuff. She said that in two years I'll be eighteen and if it's important to me I'll get it done then. She seems to understand how I feel about being flat, except she says she doesn't think I am. I think she cares about me more than Dad does, except of course she loves MG most.

Chapter Nine

Leah had two client appointments on the third Tuesday in July, and she took Mary Grace to Jodie Simon's that morning so that she could get some things done in the house. She had been to see Kassandra the day before. She was dilated to three centimeters—ripe, in other words. It was a steaming-hot day, and she'd spent the morning cleaning out the kitchen cupboards.

Leah finished her appointment with her last client of the day at three o'clock, and saw the woman out to the car where the heat seemed to be rising off every visible surface. She had fifteen minutes before Sadie's first appointment. Heading back into the house, she was surprised by the sound of the piano. Scott Joplin.

She opened the door and saw Camille sitting at the piano. "Camille," she said as the teenager stopped playing. "I didn't know you played."

"I took Suzuki method when I was little, when we lived with Dad. Then, I took some in California, but I stopped. It's kind of late for me to do anything with it."

"You play well," Leah said. Possibly better than she herself did. "Would you like to take lessons again?"

Camille shrugged. She had gone out by herself the day before and come back with her head shaved and one piercing through her left eyebrow and another through her belly button. Mark had eventually gotten out of her that she'd used a fake California ID at the tattoo parlor downtown to prove that she was eighteen.

Camille had refused to see a counselor—so far at least. But she had listened to Leah's argument that a counselor would be someone on *Camille's* side, her advocate. She'd said she'd think about it. To Leah, the rebellion of the hair and the piercings was Camille's way of telling her father—and probably her mother and stepfather as well—that there were choices no one else could stop her from making.

Strangely, the loss of her hair seemed to make Camille even more striking, accentuating the beautiful bones of her face, her finely shaped jaw.

Leah left Camille sitting at the piano and slipped into the kitchen to take lemonade out of the freezer. She'd been making fresh lemonade every day and couldn't seem to get enough of it, especially now when her stomach was a little queasy. "Want some lemonade?" she asked Camille.

Camille abandoned the piano and came into the kitchen just as Leah felt an enormous surge and release in her abdomen and water rushed down between her legs, splattering the newly cleaned floor.

"God," Camille said, eyes round. She stared at Leah, shocked.

Leah said, "Please call your dad while I call Kassandra."

"Are you going to have the baby?" Camille said, frozen on the spot.

"Yes," Leah said. Her cell phone lay on the kitchen counter, and she reached for it.

Camille regained the ability to move and hurried toward her room to get her own phone.

Kassandra did not answer, and so Leah paged her, knowing that the midwife would guess she was in labor and come. She heard Camille saying, "Dad, come home. Leah's going to have the baby. Bye."

So Camille hadn't been able to reach her father, either.

Camille came back into the kitchen and gazed at Leah again, as though both mesmerized and terrified. Leah knew Camille was feeling the power of the vortex of birth, a force stronger than any human. Camille said, "Do you want me to do something? Tell me what to do. Shouldn't you lie down?"

Leah shook her head, acknowledging the contraction. "The sheets. They're in a plastic bag in the bedroom closet." Sterilized in a hot dryer, prepared for the birth. Sheets to cover the bedroom rug, too.

She followed Camille into the bedroom in a daze, working on autopilot because Mary Grace's birth had gone so slowly, and this was beginning so fast. The contractions seemed powerful, overwhelming. But they might be that way for hours. "Did you call the Wilderness Challenge number as well as his cell phone?" she asked.

The doorbell rang, and Leah thought that no one ever used the doorbell and then remembered Sadie. "Can you get that?"

"Yes, yes. No, I just left a message on his cell phone, I'll call them." Camille's voice, all a rush, drifted back to Leah as she hurried to the door.

Leah heard the teenager saying something to the newcomer, undoubtedly Sadie. Then, the seventeen-year-old appeared in the bedroom door. "Leah, are you doing this by yourself?" Sadie asked.

Camille pushed past Leah's client into the bedroom and resumed removing the patchwork quilt from the bed.

"That wasn't the plan," Leah said. "I'm sorry about this. We'll have to reschedule." She began to laugh, and the next contraction began as a tickling sensation up the spine and built to that force beyond control, heaving within her, pushing.

With hands freshly scrubbed in the bathroom, she touched between her legs and was alarmed to feel the baby's head.

Camille and Sadie seemed to be working in silent, awestruck harmony, making the bed. Camille said, "Should I boil water or something?"

"My midwifery bag," Leah said in a dazed breath as she watched the second hand on the wall clock. *This is crazy.*

Camille brought the bag to the bed.

"And wash your hands."

"I'll call Wilderness Challenge."

"Just wash your hands," Leah said.

MARK BROKE the speed limit, but no patrol car saw or stopped him. There was no need to hurry. Her last labor had been long.

But he hurried.

He had just yelled at Jason, "It's Leah. The baby."

Jason, on his cell phone in his office, hadn't seemed to hear or care.

Mark didn't bother to call the house, focused only on driving.

There was a strange car in the driveway, an old Mazda with a single bumper sticker: My Other Car Is a Pair of Boots.

He turned off the ignition and jumped out of his truck in one motion. He opened the front door and hurried through to the bedroom, stopping abruptly in the doorway.

His bald daughter and another girl, who looked as Gothic as a vampire, were with Leah, who squatted on the floor, holding the rocking chair in still balance, her face flushed, her eyes bright and wild.

"I don't think the cord's around the neck," Camille said, gloved hands on the wet dark thing hanging between Leah's legs. "I'm sure it's not."

The other girl wore gloves, too.

Leah saw Mark as she gave one push that released the baby from her in a stinging mass, a moan leaving her lips. She dropped her eyes to the baby boy, purplish-red, screwing up its face as Sadie turned him carefully.

"The placenta," Leah told Camille, who left the baby to Sadie to look at Leah and nod.

"Do I need to do anything?"

I can't hemorrhage. "Not unless there's a lot of bleeding. I'll tell you."

"What do I do then?"

"Massage my uterus. Get shepherd's purse."

Camille threw a glance toward the opened mid-wifery bag.

Mark stepped into the room.

"Wash your hands," Camille snapped at him.

But instead he knelt beside Leah and gazed at his son.

"He's beautiful," the Gothic girl said.

Mark took him from her carefully. He glanced at Camille, but his daughter was looking at Leah, looking worried and vigilant and fierce. *How did she do this?* he thought and looked at the baby again.

"I'm Sadie," the Goth told him.

"Mark," he replied, seeing his chin and a nose he was sure would be like his. He lifted his eyes to Leah's, but she was busy kneeling, groaning slightly, and then the placenta came.

KASSANDRA was there, had checked the newborn and Leah, brewed an infusion for the latter to ward off bleeding. The boy tried to find his mother's nipple.

Mark had never felt so deeply in love with Leah, so determined to protect her. And his daughter suddenly seemed a stranger to him, a person with piercings and no hair who had just attended the birth of her half brother. There was no noticeable rapport between her and Sadie. They had just met over this incredibly fast birth, had barely exchanged names, were both awestruck.

Camille sat gingerly on the edge of the bed beside Leah.

Leah said suddenly, "Mary Grace."

"I'll go get her," Mark said.

"No, call Jodie. Someone can bring her."

"I'll go get her," Sadie offered.

"Thank you," Leah and Mark said as one. And then Leah looked at Camille and said what she'd already said once: "Thank you. You were amazing."

Camille said, "I guess he's my brother." She squinted thoughtfully. "Kind of wild, when I consider how he came to be."

"Yes," Leah agreed with a quiet laugh.

"What are you going to call him?" Camille asked.

Mark looked at Leah, but her eyes were all on the baby again.

Camille had looked at the baby names Mark and Leah had considered. "I like Matthew. Matthew James."

Leah lifted her eyes to Mark, gauging his reaction.

His expression was questioning, seeking her agreement.

She gave a nod.

"Matthew James Logan he is," Mark said.

He had latched on to Leah's nipple.

Kassandra continued unobtrusively tidying the bedroom, watching over mother and child.

When Sadie returned with Mary Grace, Camille was sitting in the rocker holding Matthew on her knees.

"Is that my brother?" Mary Grace shouted.

"Quiet," Mark said automatically.

Camille's voice was gentler. "We have to be quiet

for the baby, Mary Grace." Carefully she lifted the infant into her arms and scooted over in the rocker. "Sit with me, and I'll help you hold him."

Leah gazed at the two girls with love, wondering at how it had occurred through the birth of Matthew James; Camille was her daughter, too, precious and irreplaceable. She moved carefully on the bed. She had torn some during the birth, twenty stitches' worth, which Kassandra had taken care of.

Mark sat beside her, one hand on his ankle, studying Camille and Mary Grace and Matthew. His daughter surprised him with her maturity.

"He's cute," Mary Grace told Camille, looking up at the teenager appealingly. Then she reached up and touched the ring through Camille's eyebrow, as though fascinated by it.

"We shouldn't touch it," Camille said, "because it can get infected that way."

Again, Mark was impressed by his daughter's maturity and patience. Had the birth changed her? *Stupid question, Mark.*

Of course it had.

It had changed all of them.

They were a family now.

But Mary Grace hadn't been there, and Mark realized, not for the first time, that the four-year-old was going to prove the test of his own strength in his relationship with Leah.

"Camille and Sadie did everything but the stitches," Leah concluded, watching her sister hold Matthew. As soon as they heard about the birth, Ellen and River had rushed over to meet their new nephew.

This show of caring, of love, from her sister soothed and pleased Leah. "Thank you for coming," she said softly.

"He looks like Mark," Ellen said with a little laugh, a slightly brittle laugh.

"I think so, too."

River had admired Matthew and was now out in the living room tuning Mark's guitar, trying it out.

"Everything works out perfectly for you," Ellen said.

Leah stared at Ellen. "Like my husband dying?"

Ellen shrugged. "Now you have Mark. And another perfect child."

Damn it, Ellen. Can't you ever be thankful for what you have?

Leah said, "I feel very fortunate." She watched Matthew's tiny mouth blow a bubble.

"You had a girl, and now you have a boy, too."

"Soon you'll have two boys," Leah said. "You look beautiful, Ellen." Some women pregnant with twins quickly became huge and always seemed uncomfortable. Not Ellen. Perhaps it was her daily yoga practice or her healthy diet that kept her complexion blooming and her body trim.

Ellen said, "I like being pregnant. I'm a manifestation of divine femininity."

With a smile, Leah said, "I can't argue. You're going to be a perfect earth mother."

For a moment, a glimpse in time, she saw her sister as she would be as the mother of twins and knew she had spoken truly. Ellen seemed to see herself that way, too, embraced her own power for that moment, a pregnant woman holding a newborn, an embodiment of fertility, nurturing, beauty and joy.

Then, the curtain closed. "The perfect earth mother who gives birth in a hospital," Ellen said.

Leah had spoken with Kassandra and Dr. Holmes about Ellen's pregnancy. They had come up with a plan and agreed that Leah should be the one to broach it. She was still her sister's midwife.

"We've come up with an idea," she said tentatively, afraid of Ellen's unreasonableness. She did not want to deal with her little sister's attitude today. "I talked to Kassandra, as you said I could, and to Dr. Holmes. Kassandra has handled a lot of births at her home in Delta, and she has a birthing tub there. We're willing to try it there, if you carry the twins to thirty-six weeks. She's literally a block from the hospital."

Ellen gazed at her, and Leah knew that her fears that her sister would not appreciate this alternative were groundless.

She said, "Oh, God, that would be great. And you'll both be there, you and Kassandra."

"Yes, and she'll discuss the fees with you and River. She'd like to oversee your care, if that's all right. It was the compromise," Leah said, though it had been no compromise as far as she was concerned. There were so many sibling issues between her and Ellen that this was a better solution.

"Okay," Ellen said. "Okay. Oh, God, I know I've got to hang on to them."

Not go into early labor, she meant.

Leah did not want to say that many women carrying twins did not carry for as long as thirty-six weeks. Ellen knew these things. She'd been reading about pregnancy and birth since long before she'd conceived.

"Danine's going to be at the birth," Ellen said.

Leah just nodded. She didn't care for Danine, but Ellen did. And who would be at the birth was Ellen and River's choice. Leah knew that her sister had read books by Michel Odent, who advocated a quiet atmosphere and a single birth attendant. If the mother was disturbed as little as possible, she could go into the trancelike state most conducive to birth. Leah had to admit that Camille and Sadie had been model attendants in this respect, both focused on her and often silent, their only conversations both quiet and necessary.

Leah cherished the joy around her now, the recent memory of her labor supported by those two young women.

The conversation was interrupted by a wail from the living room. Mary Grace.

She shrieked, "No! My mom's going to make macaroni and cheese."

Camille's soft voice, explaining something to Mary Grace. Mark's less yielding voice.

"I hate you! You should go away!" Mary Grace's footsteps running toward the master bedroom.

Mark saying, "Mary Grace, come back here."

Leah knew Mark wanted to protect her from becoming too tired, but this was a time when Mary Grace needed reassurance, not harsh discipline.

Her daughter's tear-streaked face appeared in the doorway, and Mary Grace hurled herself at the bed.

"Careful, sweetheart," Leah said.. "Would you like to come up and sit beside me while I nurse Matthew?"

Mary Grace nodded, then put her thumb in her mouth and her head against Leah's side.

Mark came to the door. "Mary Grace," he said, "please come here. I'd like you to go to your room and spend some time there quietly. Then we can talk."

Mary Grace shook her head, pressing herself closer to Leah.

Ellen got up and left the room, saying something about asking River what they were doing for dinner. They'd brought food for Leah's family, food that had been rejected by Mary Grace.

Leah simply wanted to sit with her daughter and son, enjoying them both. She told Mark, "Mary Grace just wants to enjoy her brother."

"Yes," said Mary Grace, sitting up and glaring at Mark.

Mark said, "Yes, but I think she needs to do some thinking and apologizing first."

Mary Grace ignored him and looked at the baby, who had dropped off, exhausted.

Leah said, "He's going to sleep now, Mary Grace, and I'm going to lie here with him."

"I want macaroni and cheese."

"I think Mark just said he'd make you some."

"I want you to do it."

Leah said, "Sweetie, this is one day when Mom really needs to rest. So please be a big girl and let Mark make your dinner."

"Camille can make it," Mary Grace said, glowering.

Mark tried to separate himself from the equation. It wasn't personal that Leah's daughter sometimes behaved as though she hated him—indeed, had just told him so. But he had to think about what was right for the child, and letting her get her way right now wasn't it.

"I'm going to make it," he said, "and you can decide whether or not to eat."

"I don't like you," Mary Grace said.

"Mary Grace, that's not nice."

Mary Grace picked at a thread on the quilt that covered her mother. She said, "I want to sleep in here tonight. With you and my brother."

Mark walked away, left the doorway, strode into the kitchen, banged a pot on the stove to begin the macaroni and cheese he knew would not be eaten, might be thrown on the floor, and then stilled and took a breath.

Camille said, "I can make it, Dad."

"That's not what's needed." He looked at her, feeling warmth, happiness for all she'd done that day. "But thank you. I'm so proud of you. You were a heroine today."

Camille flushed. "Thanks. I'm going to see if Leah needs help."

"Thank you," he repeated.

He wanted suddenly to hold his new son again, to smell his skin. But he did not want to return to the room where Mary Grace reigned as Brat in Chief. He did, however, wander into the hall outside the bedroom, listening.

"It hurts people's feelings when you say you hate them," Leah was saying.

"I didn't hurt his feelings," Mary Grace insisted.

"I would like you to say that you're sorry, Mary Grace."

"I'm not sorry."

"Sometimes we have to apologize even when we're not really sorry."

"Can I sleep in here?"

A sigh. "Yes."

Mark wanted to swear. He knew that Mary Grace's crawling into her mother's bed had been a frequent occurrence before he appeared in their lives. Twice, she had even joined the two of them, curling up on her mother's side once and between them on the other occasion. Neither incident had really bothered him. He liked Mary Grace—well, wanted to like her—and he wanted her to like him. And he'd certainly climbed into his own parents' bed as a small child, had often slept with them.

He returned to the kitchen and made macaroni and cheese, confident that Mary Grace would not eat it, that Leah would make allowances for her and finally get up herself to make a snack for her daughter. They had been there before in different ways. He hated it. He was a man, the man of the house, becoming a father to Mary Grace, and yet Leah seemed never to support his decisions in regard to the child.

He didn't want to argue with Leah, but he did want to protect her, did not want to see her harassed by a willful four-year-old. She'd just had a baby, after all.

Yes, Leah was an adult. Yes, it was her choice. But Mary Grace's behavior affected everyone in the house.

Also, most importantly, Mark didn't think it was good for Mary Grace to get her way by destroying the peace of the entire household.

The evening went much as he'd anticipated, except that Mary Grace fell asleep before the macaroni and cheese was done and would not be awakened, not until 11:00 p.m. when she awoke Leah and asked Leah to make her a snack.

Mark offered to make her a snack—making the decision for the greater imperative, that Leah should be able to nurse Matthew and go back to sleep. Mary Grace agreed, and he made her a peanut butter and jelly sandwich and summoned the energy to thank her for helping her mother by being so grown up and letting him make the sandwich.

Then, Matthew had finished nursing but was still crying, so Mark took the newborn and walked with him.

Mary Grace went to her own bed and went to sleep.

Paonia, Colorado
Camille's journal

Dear Diary,

Dad and MG have a nonstop war of wills. I think he and Leah are going to split up because of it. Leah lets MG get away with murder, and Dad hates that, and they're having shouting matches about it, and Matthew, I guess, wakes up a lot at night.

I love taking care of him, but now Dad can't keep a relationship together either. It's a good thing he and Leah aren't married because they'd probably just end up divorced.

It's August, and Mom has been in France for two weeks, and she hasn't called once. She's always busy going to screenings and parties with her boyfriend or whatever he is, according to the short e-mails she manages to whip off.

Tish called. Her life is so different from mine. I mean, her parents are divorced, too, but she always has plenty of money and nobody tries to stop her doing things because of the *principle* of the thing. Mom sends me money, but I know Dad's angry about it. He wants everyone to be treated alike, and he says Mary Grace isn't going to get a lot of money just given to her and same with Matthew. Oh, well! Does he think I'm, like, going to tell her not to send it? And she says she'll buy me a car. I think she probably gives me enough money to pay the insurance, because Dad says he won't. Also, he says I need his permission to get a license. Same big deal. It's not fair for me to have someone buy me my own car when that won't happen for MG or Matthew. I had driver training in California, but he doesn't seem to think that matters. Leah isn't as into *principles* as he is. She and I get along fine, even though I think she lets MG act like a brat sometimes.

I bet the school here sucks, and I told Dad, but like he cares? He's after me to take piano lessons again. I don't know. Sometimes things seem so pointless. I'm trying to figure out what kind of car I want. Mom says I can get something new but that I should probably think about gas mileage. Um, yeah?

Chapter Ten

"We can still go to Breckenridge," Leah told Camille. "I promised you I'd take you." To shop. It was the last week before Labor Day, and Leah wanted to do everything she could to make Camille happy and self-confident for the start of school.

She and Camille sat on the living-room couch together. Camille had been looking at clothes in copies of *Elle* and *Vogue* that she'd bought that week.

Camille said, "Everybody dresses so differently here, though." She was waiting with Leah for Sadie to arrive for her prenatal appointment. Then, she would watch Matthew while Leah saw the pregnant seventeen-year-old. After Sadie's appointment, Leah would go collect Mary Grace from Jodie Simon's house.

Leah was nursing Matthew. She put her finger on her nipple beside his mouth to break suction and switch breasts. But the timing was awry, the milk still pumping, and a thin jet of milk doused his face, then, as she moved him, shot a dozen feet across the room to hit the window.

"My God!" said Camille. "I can't I believe I just saw that."

Feeling a certain satisfaction in hearing this observation from Camille, Leah stopped the flow with a clean cotton diaper and moved Matthew to her other breast. She laughed. "That's how I feel about it, too."

Camille said, "I never thought of breasts as something that could—well, *do* something like that. Sadie told me there was some woman who was stranded and kept her husband and children alive with her breast milk."

"Husband, too, eh?" Leah said.

Camille shrugged.

"In many less-developed places," Leah agreed, "women nurse their children for much longer."

"Because food's not so available?" Camille asked.

"Yes. Probably for cultural reasons, too." Cautiously, Leah asked, "Are you still upset about the surgery?" About Mark's not allowing it.

"I wish I had bigger breasts." Camille shrugged.

"And I'll be glad when mine are smaller again," Leah said firmly. "Though I like nursing. I love nursing babies."

Camille said, "Maybe I should tell Dad I'll just get pregnant and get big breasts that way."

Leah groaned, imagining Mark's reaction.

"He'd probably just find some dungeon for me," Camille said.

Probably, Leah thought. Mark often seemed to think that the only way to create the world he wanted was by the imposition of authority. The result: Camille was quickly honing manipulation to an art form. And Mary Grace was becoming a person who sought allies with a sort of divide-and-conquer strategy. Not that Leah believed Mary Grace understood what she was doing. But Mark wanted both girls to abide by his rules, and Mary Grace, in particular, responded with equal determination, seeking to get her way.

Leah was the only one in the household who argued with Mark with what she considered grown-up ethics. She found it exhausting.

The problem was, Mark's position had traditional wisdom behind it. He argued against anything that he thought might "spoil" any of the children. Leah, however, could see the downside of authoritarian systems. She wanted her children—and she included Camille in this number—to know that they *did* have the power to get what they wanted by honest methods. Yes—no one got every desire met every time. But a person who was always told no either learned to seek her aims by devious means or, worse, to believe that she could *not* achieve what she wanted. Leah didn't want this for Camille, Mary Grace or Matthew.

Also, she had a strong feeling that Mark's power struggles with Camille and Mary Grace were minor skirmishes compared to the warfare he might someday experience with a teenage son.

The doorbell rang, and Camille held out her arms for Matthew.

Leah handed her son to Camille. "Thank you."

She paid Camille for watching Matthew and sometimes Mary Grace. Camille never refused the money, and Leah saw in that both a healthy desire to earn and an unvoiced fear that Mark would someday succeed in stopping the money that Sabrina put into the teenager's bank account.

Finally, nearly a month after Matthew's birth, Sadie Keller was having her first prenatal appointment with Leah.

In the master bedroom where Sadie had attended Matthew's birth, Leah now took the teenager's history and learned more about the circumstances of the pregnancy.

"Lucas Reed?" Sadie said, answering questions about the child's father. "He goes to Mesa State.

"He's in a nursing program, now," Sadie said. "He's planning to be an RN. We want to live together, but it makes more sense now for him to live up there and me to be down here."

"You're going to finish school?" Leah asked. Sadie was starting her senior year at Paonia High School.

"Yeah. I only have to go half time, though. And I'm going to take dance classes at Mesa State."

"That will probably help with the birth," Leah agreed. Women who exercised regularly, particularly forms of exercise with stretching, seemed to have easier and more trouble-free labors than those who did not. But more dramatic was the difference in how the babies of these mothers seemed. Very, very pink and healthy, with higher Apgar scores.

She and Sadie talked for twenty minutes about the specific nutritional needs of teenage mothers, and Leah was pleased to find that the girl, on her own initiative, had invested in an excellent brand of prenatal vitamins.

When Leah addressed the subject of payment, Sadie told her firmly that she would cover her own expenses. "I mean, I get a free place to live from my mom, and she buys food. Well, we get a lot from the garden and the restaurant. But I support myself otherwise. I pay for everything. None of us has medical insurance, anyway. It's too expensive."

Leah wondered if she'd ever hear the words "It's too expensive," from Camille Logan, but it was only a passing question. She had no doubt that Camille possessed the backbone she would need to survive in the world, whatever life threw at her. Also, it was unfair to compare a teenager who'd spent most of her life living in affluence in Laguna Beach to Sadie Keller, who seemed to Leah to have remarkable inner resources which she'd needed to use early in life.

It was Sadie who made the comparison, obliquely and yet obviously. She seemed to see through the walls of the house to wherever Camille and Matthew were as she said, "I mean, I've never had a clothing allowance or anything like that, and my mom doesn't buy me clothes now. I go to thrift stores." She shrugged, with not a little pride.

Leah said, "I do, too. Be sure to wash everything in hot water and dry it in a hot dryer, though, when you bring it home. They did have a lice outbreak at one of the stores in Delta, and it's very hard—let me say, almost impossible—to get rid of lice and mites without insecticides that we don't want you using now."

"Got it."

Sadie drew her eyebrows together and, with a slight

sneer, indicated Camille Logan, somewhere in the house. "Has she ever, like, had a job?"

Leah was not about to criticize Camille to Sadie. "She's doing one right now," she replied, thinking gratefully of how good Camille was with Matthew. Since participating in Matthew's birth, Camille had forged a particularly strong bond with the infant and never seemed put out when asked to care for him.

"I mean, she's never had to earn money, has she?" Sadie asked.

Leah pretended total concentration on her appointment book, flipping pages and squinting at her own writing, then trying to draw ink from a perfect functional ballpoint pen. "Let's see. I should see you again in about four weeks…"

Sadie seemed to understand that she wasn't going to get any satisfaction from Leah on the subject and dropped it.

"Why don't you take her to Grand Junction to shop?" Mark asked that evening. "She can go to the mall like everyone else."

I hate going to the mall, Leah reflected. "I promised her Breckenridge, and I want to take her there."

"You had a baby less than a month ago," he pointed out. "Isn't it going to exhaust you?"

"The drive's only a couple of hours, and I'm sure Camille will help with Matthew," Leah said. "She always does, Mark. It sounds like a cliché, but I don't know where I'd be without her."

Mark studied Leah's face and recognized the truth

of her words. While he didn't think Camille should be paid for babysitting—not when she already got so much money from her mother—he recognized that his daughter made Leah's life much easier.

Finally, he let it go. He had enough to think about. Jason was out of the country again. Jason had offered to sell him the business, but for the time being Mark was content to act as manager. With Jason's approval, he had just hired another counselor, this one with a master's degree and experience counseling adolescent boys.

As Leah was putting Mary Grace to bed, the four-year-old said, "Can I go to Breckenridge?"

"No," Mark said from the doorway.

Leah told her, "You'd be bored. Long car trip and then lots of shopping."

"I like it there," Mary Grace said, and Leah remembered that she and Mary Grace had gone there the previous winter, for a regional midwifery conference. She was surprised Mary Grace remembered it so well.

"But it's a special time I've promised Camille," Leah said.

Camille had paused in the doorway beside her father. "It's okay with me."

"How would you like to come to work with me?" Mark said. He had taken Mary Grace to work with him twice, but only for a couple of hours at a time, and although he'd given her small tasks to do and paid her for them she'd quickly grown bored.

"I want to go to Breckenridge," Mary Grace said.

This time, Mark could see that Leah didn't want to

take the four-year-old, and he was relieved. But incredibly he heard her say, "Okay. You'll be bored, though."

"No, I won't," Mary Grace replied. "I'll be good."

Mark knew the trip was doomed to be exhausting for Leah. But she had chosen it.

Angry, trying not to let that anger show, he turned away from the doorway and headed for the front door.

WHEN HE RETURNED to the house, Camille was curled up on the couch watching a movie with the sound on low.

Mark glanced at the screen. "What is it?"

"Sleepless in Seattle."

He had a feeling he was going to be sleepless in Paonia tonight. He said, "Will you turn off the lights?"

"Yes. Good night."

The bedroom light was off, Leah and Matthew asleep. Neither stirred as he got into bed. He wasn't surprised. Leah was so tired these days that he sometimes had to wake her when Matthew was wailing beside her, hungry. Leah had admitted that she sometimes dreamed she was nursing him, only to awaken in surprise to find him still crying.

Damn Mary Grace.

But it wasn't Mary Grace's fault. It was Leah's fault. Yes, Mary Grace could make a royal stink when she didn't get her own way. And she often got her way. Mark wasn't sure which way the cause and effect worked on that one, it all seemed so wrong to him. Had Leah always given in to her this way? His initial experience of Mary Grace had been that she was an attractive, intelligent, well-behaved child.

His current perception was that she was spoiled but her attitude would probably turn around after a week of normal discipline. A screaming fit? She could go have it in her bedroom. Rudeness? She could go to her room until she was ready to apologize and behave politely.

He loved Leah, was committed to Leah. But he could not live in a home ruled by a four-year-old's desires.

Unfortunately, he knew that Leah, nursing a four-week-old and caring for midwifery clients, plus her sister, did not need grief from him.

THE TRIP to Breckenridge was pleasant, Leah decided. With Camille's company and intermittent attention, Mary Grace was less whiny than she might otherwise have been. Camille found some clothes she liked and bought a stuffed manatee for Mary Grace.

Nonetheless, Leah insisted they head for home by four-thirty, and when they returned to the house, all she could do was drop onto the bed and sleep.

She awoke with the sheet beneath her blood-soaked. Mark had just come into the room, switching on the bathroom light, which normally wouldn't have awakened her.

When she sat up, he came over to kiss her and look down at Matthew, sleeping beside her.

He saw the blood. "What's your physician's number?"

Leah glanced at the clock. Eight-thirty. "You can call

Kassandra." Though she knew what to do. Shepherd's purse, nurse Matthew and rest.

Rest.

She said, "I guess I did too much."

He found the midwife's number on a sheet beside the bed, dialed and handed the phone to Leah, then sat gently beside her, frightened. He knew women bled for a while after birth, but he had thought Leah's bleeding had tapered off. He had to remind himself what a lot of blood looked like, and this wasn't it. It *did* look like more than Leah should be losing today though.

He got a towel for her and placed another on her rocker. "Can you sit here? I'll change the sheets."

Leah picked up Matthew and did as he suggested.

Kassandra answered, and Leah told her everything, including how she'd spent the day. Kassandra made the same suggestions she herself would have made, adding, "Really—take it easy, Leah."

"I will," Leah promised.

As she hung up, Mark, in the midst of changing sheets, eyed her quizzically. She told him everything Kassandra had said and waited for him to tell her that she shouldn't have gone to Breckenridge—*or* that she shouldn't have taken Mary Grace along. He didn't. He just made the bed, fluffing her pillow, and took Matthew from her when she finished nursing.

"You're kind of wet, aren't you, buddy?" he said, taking him to the changing table.

Gratefully, Leah made her way to the bathroom and, minutes later, climbed between the clean sheets. She fell asleep with Matthew beside her, nursing again, and Mark's arms around her, his front warming her back.

Mark lay awake with the certain knowledge that life in this house had to change. The decision made finally allowed him to sleep.

Paonia, Colorado
Camille's journal

Dear Diary,

James called! From LB. I am so blown away. He said he saw Tish yesterday and she'd told him about Mom and Glenn and he'd wanted to say he was sorry I wasn't coming back and he wanted to know how I liked Colorado. He's been to Paonia! For some music festival.

Anyhow, I told him about Matthew and the birth and everything, and he was way more interested than Tish was. I told him about my hair, and he wants me to e-mail him a picture. My laptop came with the boxes Glenn sent, but I haven't set it up yet. Leah has e-mail, high-speed unbelievably.

James said he's been learning to surf, that's all. He's also really into marine biology, I guess. He told me about seeing dolphins. I told him he'll see more, and whales, in the winter. I don't know what I'm excited about, because he lives there and I'm stuck here.

Chapter Eleven

Mary Grace said, "I want to stay at home with Mom and Camille and Matthew."

Camille shrugged as though to say it was okay with her.

Mark said, "You have a choice, Mary Grace. You can come to work with me, or you can go to Jodie Simon's."

Leah heard the argument from the bedroom. Matthew was awake and she had been enjoying lying in bed, looking at him while he gazed back at her.

A wail erupted in the next room.

Mary Grace was insecure again, wanting to be close to her. Well, Leah was going to be home all day, resting. She called, "Mark."

Instead, Mary Grace's feet thumped the floor as she ran toward the bedroom. But the running stopped, and instead Mary Grace began to scream. Mark said, "Your mother is resting. You're not to disturb her."

Mary Grace continued great hiccupping sobs, shrieks that tore through the house.

"Mark!" Leah called, annoyed.

She heard him at Mary Grace's door. "You can stay there until you stop crying or until I come and get you to take you to Jodie's or to work with me."

Kicking. The wall. The door. "Mom! Mom!" The door opening.

"Mary Grace, I said stay."

"No! You don't make the rules."

"Actually, I do."

Leah put Matthew in his bassinet and came out into the hall in her nightgown.

Mary Grace ran to her, sobbing.

Leah asked Mark, "What's going on?"

"I've told Mary Grace that she's going to Jodie's or to work with me."

"She can stay—"

"No, she can't. Mary Grace, go back to your room."

"No!"

Mark plucked Mary Grace from beside Leah's legs, and Mary Grace shrieked, an earsplitting sound.

Leah demanded, "Don't you understand what's going on?"

He deposited Mary Grace in her room and shut the door again.

"I understand that you're tired and that a four-year-old is trying to make the rules in this house."

"She has a new brother, a new older sister and a new father," Leah exclaimed. "That's a lot to cope with."

With a glance at Camille, Mark walked toward Leah, guided her back into their bedroom, and shut the door.

Mary Grace's shrieks, kicking and sobbing, still

sounded like a wailing siren through the house. Matthew began to cry, and Leah hurried to pick him up.

The bedroom door opened and Mary Grace came in.

Mark crossed the room, picked her up and endured her kicking and shrieks as he carried her back to her bedroom.

Leah said, "Mark, don't. What is it, honey?"

Mark set the girl on the floor and glowered.

"I want to stay home with you."

"You may stay home with me. Now run along to your room so Mark and I can talk."

Mary Grace sniffed. "Okay." She went slowly out of the room. Leah heard her daughter's door open and shut.

Mark closed their bedroom door, then turned to Leah. "I'm not living in a household that's ruled by a four-year-old tyrant."

"She's not a tyrant."

"She's becoming one."

"Can't you see," Leah hissed, "she's insecure because of Matthew and because of you? She needs patience."

"She needs limits."

Leah shrugged. "I warned you."

Mark gaped at her. "What are you talking about?"

"That we might not get along."

"You and I get along fine."

"Yes, but I'm not going to let you be a dictator."

"I think I make a better dictator than your four-year-old daughter does, actually."

"Mark, can't you see? I just talked with her. I persuaded her. I communicated with her."

"Actually, you gave in to her. That's why she stopped crying."

Leah, on the verge of tears, tears of exhaustion, sat down. Matthew continued to fuss.

Mark said, "You're exhausted. Last night you woke up in a pool of blood."

"It was a little bleeding. I just did too much."

"Exactly. Which is why I want Mary Grace with me or at Jodie's today. Does she act like this when you have to go to a birth?"

"She's never acted like this until you came on the scene and started acting like the king of the castle."

Mark slowed his breathing. He took Matthew, held him against his shoulder. *I have to stick this out. I have to make it work.* He didn't know how. He could offer to stay home, but if Mary Grace was also in the house it would mean more clashes, more power struggles. He'd learned with Sabrina that ultimatums led to the sudden death of a relationship.

"What's wrong with saying no to her once in a while?" he finally asked.

"It's not that you're saying no. It's that she doesn't understand why. If there's no reason to say no to her, then she's going to see it as unfair."

"The reason," he said, "is so that you can rest and recover from Matthew's birth. You're a midwife, Leah. What would you do if you saw one of your clients' children exhausting her?"

"Mary Grace doesn't exhaust me. It's your fighting with Mary Grace that exhausts me."

"Leah, she's becoming a spoiled brat." The words

were out, he firmly believed them to be true, and he knew he shouldn't have said them.

"If you can't love and respect my daughter, you and I have no future."

"I respect her enough to give her limits."

"Mary Grace has always had limits! She's just never had to deal with random edicts she doesn't understand."

He had made himself a promise the night before. That promise had been to protect Leah's health because she was the woman he loved and the mother of his child. Now, he saw that resolution crumbling, suddenly looking unworkable. She would side with her daughter against him.

He knew he could not live with that situation.

"I love you, Leah."

The look in his eyes warned her, as did the words of love, and she took it all as threat, threat to her sovereignty in her own home, of her right to mother her children as she chose. His *I love you* meant *I love you; do you want to throw that love away?*

Which meant, *I love you, but I'm going to leave you if I don't get my way.*

It was, Leah felt, the wrong message.

He said, "I'm going to work. Would you like me to take Mary Grace?"

She had told Mary Grace that she could stay home. Yet she did not want to lose Mark. Mark, who routinely brought her quart jars of water when she was nursing to quench her thirst and keep her hydrated. Who *helped.* Who was a good man, just a little too authoritarian with Mary Grace.

She said, "We'll have a nice day here together."

He gazed at her for a moment, at Matthew, and then he walked out of the room and shut the door softly behind him.

He didn't say goodbye, and she wondered if he would before he left the house.

CAMILLE was in the kitchen, making herself a cup of coffee, her posture rigid.

Mark paused beside her as he pulled on his sheep-skin-lined denim jacket over his T-shirt. "Thanks for helping, Camille."

"Like it does a lot of good."

He eyed her. "What do you mean?"

She shrugged, a tense jerk. "You guys aren't going to stay together either. It's like it's not worth it for anyone."

"What's not worth it?"

"Nobody stays together. God, are all adults this selfish?"

Mark felt her words like a vise tightening down on his heart. Every fear raced through him, because Glenn and Sabrina had let down Camille, and now she believed that he was going to do the same thing.

"Whatever happens," he said, "I'm not going to abandon you, Camille."

"Just Matthew?"

"No," he said. "Nor Matthew." He said, "When you were little, you had limits, just as Mary Grace needs to have. I think you were and are better for those limits."

Camille gazed at him in disbelief. "You're fantasizing."

"What do you mean?"

"You believe that you had the answers about how to

raise me and that if I'd always lived with you I'd be a more satisfactory person."

"I think you're a great person."

"But you disapprove of the kind of life I had in Laguna Beach, a life I happened to like. You think that Mom has wrecked me by letting me make some of my own decisions."

Mark wanted to argue, to say that wasn't so.

Camille went on. "Sometimes you really don't see the forest for the trees."

"What do you mean?"

"You think that every decision you make as a parent, every limit you set, makes your children better. In fact, what it makes *me* feel is that you disapprove of me, that you don't like who I actually am. You want me to be someone else. Now, you want the same thing for Mary Grace. Why can't you just love us the way we are?"

Mark stood stunned. "I do love you the way you are."

"Because I was at the birth, because I did something you approve of. It's never about love with you, just approval or disapproval."

The words stung. But were they true?

"I'm sorry you think that," was all he managed to say. "I do love you, Camille. I'm sorry you believe anything different." He scooped up his keys from the counter.

Like a taunt behind him, he heard Mary Grace's and Leah's voices in the bedroom.

LEAH LAY in bed, unhappy. Mary Grace had seemed strange after Mark left. She'd gone to play with her

Barbie dolls in her room, but Leah saw how insecure her daughter was.

When the phone rang, she looked at the caller ID and read River's and Ellen's names and number there. "Hello?"

"Hi," Ellen said, sounding relaxed, content. "I'm going to have massive pumpkins this year. They're symbolic of my hugeness."

Leah laughed in spite of herself, but Ellen seemed to hear something amiss in her voice.

"What's up, Leah? Is everything okay?"

"Not exactly. We're having some power struggles about how to parent children, exactly the kind of thing I worried about when I found out he wanted to be involved with this baby."

"Like what?"

Leah explained, telling her sister of what she saw as Mark's determination to dominate Mary Grace. "When men behave that way, they seem so weak to me."

"It sounds like he's trying to give you some space to rest, Leah."

Leah blinked, a little surprised. Ellen sounded as though she thought Leah wasn't understanding Mark's motives at all. "That's what he says. But I just can see this underlying need with him to be in charge."

"So Mary Grace should be in charge?"

Leah heard her sister's words like a bell in her head. Ellen was saying what Mark had said. It seemed so unlike Ellen to have a point of view like this. *Am I wrong?* she wondered.

"She's insecure," Leah said. "Because of Matthew."

"And probably because you're letting her do whatever she wants because of Matthew."

This remark clicked in Leah's head. Was Ellen right? It made a kind of sense. Usually, Leah told Mary Grace what was going to happen and why. Lately, Mark had been telling Mary Grace what was going to happen, Mary Grace had been arguing, and Leah had been attacking Mark to protect Mary Grace.

Ellen was saying, "I mean, gosh, he gave her a choice at least. He said she could go to work with him or to Jodie's. Where is she, anyhow?"

"Here. In her room. Playing."

And it felt wrong. It felt wrong because Mary Grace had been allowed to defy Mark, and she, Leah, had backed her daughter up.

"He probably thinks you and Mary Grace are the couple, and he's just a hanger-on."

How could her little sister be so stubborn and impulsive about some things and so…almost traditional in other ways?

When Leah ended the call, she lay on her bed and cried. Matthew slept beside her.

There was a soft tap at the bedroom door, and Leah wiped her eyes on the sheet. "Come in." She sat up, letting her hair hide part of her face, and glanced at Camille.

Camille saw the tears and seemed to freeze, very tense. "I thought I'd walk to the park with Mary Grace."

"You don't have to, Camille," Leah said. "It's going to be okay."

Camille's posture did not relax. "I just thought she'd like to get out."

Leah knew that, in fact, Camille was struggling desperately to hold together the only family she had. She made herself say, "Your dad and I are going to work it out. We're going to stay together."

The teenager didn't comment. "So is it okay if we go?"

"Yes," said Leah, knowing she had failed to reassure Camille, knowing with a feeling of despair that only time could do that.

She waited until Mary Grace had come in to hug her goodbye and to kiss her sleeping brother's cheek, beside his black hair, waited until she heard the two girls leave the house. Then, she reached for the phone and called Mark.

"Hello?"

It was not the voice he usually used to answer the phone, Leah realized. It was a tense, unfriendly tone.

And he would have read her number on the screen, known it was her.

"I just called to see—how you are. You're right about not spoiling Mary Grace. It's just that this minute maybe isn't the time to exert your authority. When she's going through so many changes."

Across town, Mark wanted nothing more than to go home, to hold her. "Well, actually—Camille made me see some things. I think maybe I remember her early childhood differently than it was." He couldn't bring himself to voice precisely what Camille had said—that perhaps he did more approving and disapproving than simply loving. He added, "And you're right about explaining things to Mary Grace instead of just laying down the law. Most of all, I think I should just try to love her as she is."

Later, as Leah hung up, she thought it would be nice if he'd said that he already did love her daughter.

But in a way, she'd never allowed him to, never allowed him to make decisions for Mary Grace that showed his love for her.

Beside her, Matthew opened his eyes.

Leah smiled at him and put one finger into his tiny hand.

Paonia, Colorado
Camille's journal

Dear Diary,

This school is really small, but this really cute guy is in my English class, and he was looking at me A LOT. Also, I'm taking a hip-hop dance class with Sadie in Junction. It's a college class, but I get P.E. credit for school. I give her some gas money. I want my license. I think I'm going to get a little Toyota hybrid when I get my license. Dad has stopped saying he won't let me get my license, and actually, he's been letting me drive to school on his way to work so I can practice.

James keeps e-mailing me. He likes my hair, he said, and he said Matthew looks like a baby! LOL. He said he might come out to New Mexico to see his grandmother for Thanksgiving, and he could take the train to Grand Junction and then use his cousin's car to drive down to New Mexico, and he could come through Paonia.

It seems like a lot of traveling for a pretty short visit with his grandmother, but they're doing a week off at Thanksgiving this year, I guess, so he'll have nine days or something.

He didn't even like me so much before, but we're really just kind of friends anyhow. E-mail friends.

Now Leah and Dad are talking about getting married at Thanksgiving. They want to do it outside here, under the oak trees. Leah wants me to be a bridesmaid.

MG will be a flower girl, of course.

Chapter Twelve

"Leah." Ellen had just signed her name in the witness spot.

In her ivory gown, a Victorian dress that Camille, Leah and Mary Grace had found at an antique store in Grand Junction, Leah glanced at her sister. They'd all come inside, Leah, Ellen, Mark, River and the minister from Paonia's most popular nondenominational church, to sign the marriage certificate at the dining-room table. Through the window, Leah could see Sadie and her boyfriend sitting on the porch swing, talking to Camille and her visiting friend, James Salazar, and another male friend from Paonia, Michael Roy, who was Sadie's cousin.

Seeing the strange almost feverish light in her sister's eyes, Leah knew. "Delta?" she said.

Ellen nodded emphatically. "I've got to call Danine."

Ellen had elected for Danine to be her labor coach.

"River can do that," Leah said.

They left in four cars. Mark was taking Mary Grace to Jodie Simon's, and he'd pick her up that evening.

Camille rode in the Subaru with Leah and Matthew, so that she could take care of the infant while Leah helped with the birth. Her friend James followed in his car, planning to go to the park with Camille and Matthew before continuing south to see his grandmother. Ellen and River rode in their car.

In the passenger seat beside Leah, who had spare clothes in the car and would change out of her wedding dress at Kassandra's house, Camille said, "This is the most bizarre wedding I've ever heard of. You guys didn't even have any champagne."

Leah laughed, shaking her head. "Your father is a very flexible man."

"I *never* thought I'd hear you say that." Camille frowned. "In fact, I've never heard anyone say that about Dad."

"But it's true," Leah admitted. After all, their honeymoon was going to be a night in Glenwood Springs, Matthew nestled between them, while Mary Grace stayed at home with Camille. Instead, that would be postponed, moved aside by Ellen's birthing. She said, "What does Michael think of James?"

"He's actually been pretty civil. Michael's so ambitious. He cares more about getting into Julliard than anything."

So it wasn't romantic between Michael and Camille. Leah had guessed as much. With James, too, Camille seemed to have an easy friendship. Her stepdaughter was so levelheaded. She had her driver's license, now. Mark had agreed to put her on his insurance on his vehicle, and Camille seemed in no hurry to get a car of her own.

Leah said, "You're really my stepdaughter now." She grinned. "That makes me so happy."

Camille returned her smile. "Thanks."

ELLEN had one of the fastest and easiest births Leah had ever attended, and the twins were born in the water and into River's hands.

Leah supported her sister's body from behind, outside the birthing tub, while Kassandra was in the tub with the parents. Leah even found herself liking Danine when she saw the woman's soothing effect on Ellen, her total concentration and support.

Holding Ellen, seeing the birth of the second boy, Leah put her head lightly against the back of her sister's. Remembering the day Ellen, on the phone, had given her such a rational opinion about Mary Grace and Mark, she said, "I love you, Ellen. There's your youngest son."

Ten minutes later, while Camille was admiring the twins and showing them to a blinking, mesmerized Matthew, Leah called Mark, got his voice mail, and left a message that the twins had been born. One was six pounds, three ounces, the other six-one.

Leah returned to the birthing room, where Ellen was now wrapped in towels on the bed. She was holding the newborns, sobbing. River sat beside her, holding her, stroking her hair.

As Leah sat in a chair beside the bed, Ellen said through her tears, "I wanted them so much. I wanted this. I can't believe it. I can't believe I have this."

Leah whispered softly, "You're a great mom, Ellen."

River and Ellen were still talking about names when Leah heard Mark's truck outside. She also heard an unexpected sound. The high voice of a little girl. "I'll be quiet. I promise. Will you carry me?"

"And the champagne?" said a deeper voice, followed by a groan of assent.

Leah closed her own eyes, which had begun to fill with tears. The front door opened and closed. Then there was a soft knock outside the door of the birthing room, and Ellen called, "Come in."

Looking up, Leah saw her husband with Mary Grace in one arm, two bottles of champagne clutched in the other hand.

I wanted this. I can't believe it. I can't believe I have this.

She said to Ellen, "Me, too."

Her sister looked up from the faces of her twin sons and met Leah's eyes with complete understanding. "I know. Mary Grace, come see your cousins."

Paonia, Colorado
Camille's journal

Dear Diary,

Forest and Gardener. It could be worse. James had already left when they were born, so I called and told him their names. He thinks it's cool. As I told Sadie, James and I will *not* be having children together. She and Lucas have decided on Benjamin Aidan, which I think is a great name. She had an ultrasound, and they found out it's a boy.

I'm going to be at her birth! I'm so flattered she wants me there.

There's my phone. It's Mom….

I'm back. She just wanted to see how I am. She wants me to come to Paris for Christmas!

And she's going to take me SHOPPING!!!!!!!

* * * * *

For the next book in our
THE STATE OF PARENTHOOD *miniseries,*
we travel to Oklahoma in Laura Marie Altom's
A DADDY FOR CHRISTMAS.
Turn the page for a sneak peak.

Chapter One

If Jess Cummings didn't act fast, the colt would have to be shot.

The heartrending sound of the young quarter horse's cries, the sight of blood staining his golden coat, made her eyes sting and throat ache. But she refused to give in to tears. For the colt's sake, for the girls' sake—most of all, for Dwayne, to whom this land and its every creature had meant so much—Jess had to stay strong.

For what felt like an eternity, while the colt's momma neighed nervously behind the broken gate the colt had slipped through, Jess struggled to free the animal from his barbed-wire cage. Muscles straining, ignoring the brutal December wind's bite, she worked on, heedless of her own pain when the barbs pierced her gloves.

"You've got to calm down," she said, praying the colt her two girls named Honey would somehow understand.

But not only didn't he stay still, he struggled all the

harder. Kicking and snorting. Twisting the metal around his forelegs and rump and even his velvety nose that her daughters so loved to stroke.

The more the vast Oklahoma plain's wind howled, the more the colt fought, the more despair in Jess's throat. It was only two days before Christmas, and the holiday would be tough enough to get through. Why, *why,* was this happening now? How many times had she spoken up at grange meetings about the illegal dumping going on in the far southeast corner of her land? How many times had she begged the sheriff to look into the matter before one of her animals—or, God forbid, children, ended up hurt? For an inquisitive colt, the bushel of rotting apples and other trash lobbed alongside hundreds of feet of rusty barbed wire had made for an irresistible challenge.

"Shh..." she crooned, though the horse fought harder and harder until he eventually lost balance, falling onto his side. "Honey, you'll be all right. Everything's going to be all right."

Liar.

Cold sweat trickled down her back as she worked, and she promised herself that this time her words would ring true. That this crisis—unlike Dwayne's—could be resolved in a good way. A happy way. A way that didn't involve tears.

From behind her came a low rumbling, and the crunch of wheels on the lonely dirt road.

She glanced north to see a black pickup approach, kicking dust up against an angry gun-metal sky. She knew every vehicle around these parts, and this one didn't belong. Someone's holiday company? Didn't matter why the traveler was there. All that truly mattered was flagging him down in time to help.

"I'll be right back," she said to Honey before charging into the road's center, frantically waving her arms. "Help! Please, help!"

The pickup's male driver fishtailed to stop on the weed-choked shoulder, instantly grasping the gravity of the situation. "Hand me those," the tall, lean cowboy type said as he jumped out from behind the wheel, nodding to her wire cutters before tossing a weather-beaten Stetson into the truck's bed. "I'll cut while you try calming him down."

Working in tandem, the stranger snipped the wire, oblivious to the bloodied gouges on his fingers and palms, as Jess smoothed the colt's mane and ears, all the while crooning the kind of nonsensical comfort she would have done to a fevered child.

In his weakened state, the colt had stopped struggling, yet his big, brown eyes were still wild.

"Call your vet?" the stranger asked.

"I would have, but I don't have a cell."

"Here," he said, standing, handing off the wire cutters. "Use Doc Matthews?"

"Yes, but—" Before she could finish her question as to how he even knew the local horse and cattle expert, the stranger was halfway to his truck. Focusing on the task at hand, she figured on grilling the man about his identity later. After Honey was out of the proverbial woods.

"Doc's on his way," the man said a short while later,

cell tucked in the chest pocket of his tan denim work jacket. "And from the looks of this little fella, the sooner Doc gets here the better."

Jess snipped the last of the wire from Honey's right foreleg, breathing easier now that the colt at least had a fighting chance. He'd lost a lot of blood, and the possibility of an infection would be a worry, but for the moment, all she could do was sit beside him, rubbing between his ears. "I can't thank you enough for stopping."

"It's what anyone would've done."

"Yes, well…" Words were hard to get past the burning knot in her throat. "Thanks."

The grim-faced stranger nodded, then went back to his truck bed for a saddle blanket he gently settled over the colt. "It's powerful cold out here. I'd like to go ahead and get him to your barn, but without the doc first checking the extent of his injuries—"

"I agree," she said. "It's probably best I wait here for him. But you go on to wherever you were headed. Your family's no doubt missing you."

His only answer was a grunt.

Turning the collar up on his jacket, eyeing her over-size coat, he asked, "Warm enough?"

"Fine," she lied, wondering if it was a bad sign that she could hardly feel her toes.

They sat in silence for a spell, icy wind pummeling their backs, Jess at the colt's head, the stranger at the animal's left flank.

"Name's Gage," he said after a while. "Gage Moore."

"J-Jess Cummings." Teeth chattering, she held out

her gloved hand for him to shake, but quickly thought better. A nasty cut, rust-colored with dried blood, ran the length of his right forefinger. His left pinkie hadn't fared much better. Both palms were crisscrossed with smaller cuts, and a frighteningly large amount of blood. "You need a doctor yourself."

He shrugged. "I've suffered worse."

The shadows behind his eyes told her he wasn't just talking about his current physical pain.

"Still. If you'd like to follow me and Doc Matthews back to the house, I've got a first-aid kit. Least I can do is bandage you up."

He answered with another shrug.

"Some of those look pretty deep. You may need stitches."

"I'm good," he said, gazing at the colt.

Jess knew the man was far from *good,* but seeing as how the vet had pulled his truck and trailer alongside them, she let the matter slide.

"Little one," the kindly old vet said to Honey on his approach, raising bushy white eyebrows and shaking his head, "you've been nothing but trouble since the day you were born."

Black leather medical kit beside him, Doc Matthews knelt to perform a perfunctory examination. He wasn't kidding about Honey having been into his fair share of mischief. He'd given his momma, Buttercup, a rough breech labor, then had proceeded along his rowdy ways to gallop right into a hornet's nest, bite into an unopened feed bag and eat himself into quite a bellyache, and now, this.

"He's going to be all right?" Jess was almost afraid to ask. "You know how attached the girls are. I don't know how I'd break it to them—"

"Don't you worry," Doc said. "This guy's tougher than he looks. I'm going to give him something for pain, have Gage help settle him and his momma in my trailer and out of this chill. Then we'll get them back to the barn so I can stitch up the little guy and salve these wounds. After that, with antibiotics and rest, he should be right as rain."

Relieved tears stung her eyes, but still Jess wouldn't allow herself the luxury of breaking down.

"How'd you get all the way out here?" Doc asked her after he and Gage gingerly placed Honey and her still-agitated momma in the horse trailer attached to the vet's old Ford. He did a quick search for Jess's truck, or Smoky Joe—the paint she'd been riding since her sixteenth birthday.

In all the excitement, Jess realized she hadn't tethered Smoky, meaning by now, he was probably back at the barn. With a wry smile, she said, "Looks like I've been abandoned. You know Smoky, he's never been a big fan of cold or Honey's brand of adventure."

"Yup." Doc laughed. "Ask me, he's the smartest one in the bunch." Sighing, heading for his pickup, Matthew's Veterinary Services painted on the doors, he said, "Oh, well, hop in the cab with me, and we'll warm up while catching up."

"Shouldn't I ride in back with the patient?"

"Relax. After the shot I gave him, he'll be happy for a while, already dreaming of the next time he gives you and I a coronary."

"Should I, ah, head back to your place?" Gage asked.

"Nope," Doc said. "Martha wanted to keep you with us till after the holidays, but I figure now's as good a time as any for you and Jess to get better acquainted."

"Mind telling me what that's supposed to mean?" Jess asked once she and Doc were in his truck. She'd removed her gloves, fastened her seat belt, and now held stiff-with-cold fingers in front of the blasting heat vents.

"What?"

"Don't act all innocent with me. You know exactly, *what.* Have you and my father been matchmaking again? If so, I—"

"Settle yourself right on down, little lady. Trust me, we learned our lesson after Pete Clayton told us you ran him off your place with a loaded shotgun."

"He tried kissing me."

"Can you blame him?" the older man said with a chuckle. "If you weren't young enough to be my granddaughter, you're pretty enough I might have a try at you myself."

Lips pursed, Jess shook her head. "Dwayne's only been gone—"

"Barely over a year. I know, Jess. We all know. But you're a bright and beautiful—very much alive—young woman with two rowdy girls to raise. Dwayne wouldn't want you living like you do, with one foot practically in your own grave."

"As usual, you're being melodramatic. Me and the girls are happy as can be expected, thank you very much. I have no interest in dating—especially not another cowboy you and my daddy come up with."

"Understood," he said, turning into her gravel drive. "Which is why Gage's only in town to help you out around the ranch."

"What?" Popping off her seat belt, she angled on the seat to cast Doc her most fearsome glare.

"Simmer down. Everyone who loves you is worried. There's too much work here to handle on your own— especially with foaling season right around the corner. We've taken up a collection, and paid Gage his first few months' wages."

She opened her mouth to protest, but before getting a word in edgewise, Doc was holding out his hand to cut off her protestations.

"While you've been off checking fences this past week, your momma and my Martha have been fixing up the old bunkhouse. Gage is a good man. I've known his family since before he was born. More importantly, he's a damned hard worker, and will considerably lighten your load."

"But, I couldn't possibly afford to—"

"Shh. Stop right there. Like I already said, whether you like it or not, the man's time has already been paid in full. Once spring rolls around and you're back on your feet after making a few sales, you'll have more than enough cash to support you and the girls and an invaluable hired hand."

Doc turned on the radio, tuning it to an upbeat country classic. Dang, but Martha had been right about Jess guessing he and her father were taking another stab at matchmaking. The wife was all the time telling him to butt out of the girl's business, but he'd never been able to turn away from a creature in need. Lord knew, Jess fell square under that category. Once he'd learned Gage was also in need of a helping hand, albeit a far different kind, he'd seen it as his civic duty to get these two lost souls together. Now, whether or not they chose to stay together was out of his hands, but in getting Gage to Jess's ranch, Doc felt better knowing he'd done his part.

"What're you grinning about?" Jess asked, shooting him a sideways glare.

"Nothin' much," Doc said, keeping his eyes on the road. "Just looking forward to the holidays."

She snorted.

"What's the matter? Someone spit in your eggnog?"

"Let's just say that the sooner this holiday season is over, the better I'll feel."

GAGE SAT in his truck's cab, wishing himself anywhere else on the planet. He'd known from the start this was a bad idea. He'd have been better off back at his cramped condo. At least there, he knew where he stood.

Though he couldn't hear words, Jess Cummings's animated body language spoke volumes. He wasn't wanted.

When his dad had first broached the subject of helping a friend of a friend up in Mercy, Oklahoma, it'd seemed like a good idea. After all, what better way to help himself than by helping others? Now, however, he realized he should have asked a helluva lot more questions about the job.

"Well?" Doc asked outside Gage's window, causing him to jump. "You gonna sit there all day, or help me get our patients to the barn?"

"Mommy!"

Gage had just creaked open his truck door when two curly-haired, redheaded munchkins dashed from the covered porch of a weary, one-story farmhouse that was in as much need of paint as it was a new tin roof. They were followed by an older, gray-haired version of Jess.

"Hey, sweeties," said Jess, the woman he'd presumed was to be his new boss, as she kneeled to catch both girls up in a hug.

The taller girl asked, "Is Honey going to be okay?"

"He'll be fine," Jess said.

"Hi." The older woman smiled warmly, extending her hand. "I'm Georgia, Jess's mom. You must be Walter's boy, Gage."

"Yes, ma'am," he said, removing the hat he'd slapped back on. It'd been a while since Gage had lived in a small town, so he'd forgotten how fast news travels. "Nice to meet you. Mom and Dad speak highly of your whole family."

"They were always favorites around here. It nearly broke my heart when your momma told me you were moving away. Of course, seeing how you were only two at the time, I'm not figuring the move gave you much cause for trouble."

"No, ma'am."

"Can you give me hand?" Doc asked from the back of his trailer.

"Sure," Gage said, secretly relieved for having been rescued from small talk. He used to love to meet new folks—or, as was apparently the case with Georgia, get reacquainted with old friends—but lately, he just didn't have the heart.

"He's bleeding!" the taller of the two girls cried at her first sight of the colt. "Mommy! Do something!" Tears streamed down the girl's cheeks while the younger girl clung to her mother's thigh, wide-eyed, with her thumb stuck in her mouth.

"Hush now," Doc said. "Honey's a tough cookie. He looks bad, but trust me, Lexie, after Gage and I get him patched up, he'll be good as new."

"Promise?"

"Yup. Now how 'bout you and Ashley get some coats on, then meet me in the barn. I could use the extra hands."

"Is it okay, Mommy?"

"Of course," Jess said. "Honey will probably be glad you two are there."

While the girls scampered inside, Georgia asked her daughter, "Now that they're busy, tell me true. Is Honey really going to be all right?"

"Doc thinks so." Even from a good twenty feet away, the exhaustion ringing from Jess's sigh struck a chord in Gage. All his father and Doc had told him was that Jess was a widow very much in need of a helping hand. No one had said anything about there being kids in the picture. Then, as if there weren't already enough needy creatures on the ranch, an old hound dog wandered up, sending a mixed message with a low growl, but tail wagging.

"Don't mind him," Jess said, jogging over. "Taffy likes letting everyone know up front who's boss. Slip him a few table scraps every now and then, and you two will be fast friends."

Georgia headed back in the house.

Gage, Doc and Jess entered the barn. While wind rattled timeworn timbers, the temperature was at least bearable compared to outside, and the air smelled good and familiar of hay and oats and leather.

The three of them managed to set the colt on a fresh straw bed in one of the stalls, then led his momma in beside him. Doc gave the colt a tap and said, "You know how Martha likes The Weather Channel. She says we're in for one heckuva storm."

"Ice or snow?" Jess asked.

"Starting off ice, switching to snow."

"Sounds fun," Jess said with a sarcastic laugh.

"Got plenty of firewood?" Doc asked.

Though she nodded, she didn't meet his gaze.

"See why I called you?" Doc asked Gage. "The girl lies through her teeth. Watch, what she calls 'plenty of wood' will be a quarter rick too wet to give good heat."

"First off," Jess said, tugging the saddled horse Gage presumed was Smoky Joe in from the paddock and into a stall, "I'm not a girl, but a woman. And second, I do have enough sense to have covered the woodpile during the last rain. Third, Gage, I know you mean well, but maybe you coming here wasn't such a good idea."

"Gage," Doc said, "whatever she blows on about, don't listen. Now, would you mind running out to my truck and getting my bag?"

"Sure," Gage said, thrilled for yet another escape.

"And after that, please check the woodpile on the south side of the house. If it's not in healthy shape, Martha will have my hide."

HANDS on her hips, after Gage was out of earshot, Jess said to Doc, "I understand you and my parents and Lord knows who else you've got in on this plan to 'save me' mean well, but seriously, Doc, I've been taking care of me and my girls just fine for a while now, and I resent like hell you and my father hiring some stranger to ride in here like a knight in shining armor."

"It's not like that," Doc said, "and kindly soften your voice. Your screech-owl-shrill tone is spooking Honey."

"Sorry," she said, "it's just that—"

"We're here," Lexie said with Ashley in tow. "What can we do?"

"Lots." Doc gave them a list of busy work that would do dual duty in not only keeping them out from underfoot, but making them feel special.

"Here's your bag," Gage said, planting it at the vet's feet. "You need anything, I'll be around the side of the house, looking after the wood."

Nibbling her lower lip, Jess gave the man a five-minute lead, then waited till Doc seemed plenty distracted with Honey's stitches before heading outside herself.

It was only two in the afternoon, but it might as well have been seven at night. The sky glowered gray.

What Jess would like to do was join her mother in the kitchen where she was no doubt nursing a pot of tea while gossiping on the phone with one of her many church friends. What Jess did instead was march around the side of the house toward her indeed lacking woodpile.

The smack-thunk of an ax splitting a log, and the halves hitting frozen ground alerted her to the fact that her new "employee" was already hard at work. Her first sight of him left her mouth dry. In a word—*wow*. Even on a day like this, splitting wood got your heat up, and Gage had removed his coat, slinging it over a split rail fence. The white T-shirt he wore hugged his powerful chest.

Fighting an instant flash of guilt for even thinking such a thing, she averted her gaze before saying, "Put your coat back on before you catch your death of cold."

He glanced up, his breath a fine, white cloud. "I'm plenty warm. How's Honey?"

"Better. Doc's working on his stitches. Looks like he'll be here a while, but for sure, the worst has passed."

"Honey's a lucky fella," Gage said, mid smack into another log, "that you came along when you did. How'd you even know to look for him all the way out there?"

"He's always been fascinated by that old trash pile. When he and his mom went missing, that's the first place I thought to look."

"Some of that trash didn't look so old." He reached for another log, causing his biceps to harden. Again, Jess found herself struggling to look away.

"No. That valley's always been a favorite dump site. Not sure why—or how—I'll ever stop folks from using it."

He grunted.

It'd been so long since she'd been around a man not old enough to be her father or grandfather, she wasn't sure what the cryptic, wholly masculine reply meant. Maybe nothing. A catchall for the more wordy, feminine version of, *It's amazing how downright rude some people can be by littering on a neighbor's land.*

"You, um, really should put your coat back on," she said, telling herself her advice had nothing to do with the fact the mere sight of that T-shirt clinging to his muscular chest was making her pulse race. "Looks like freezing rain could start any minute."

Again, she got the grunt.

"Freezing rain's nothing to mess around with," she prattled on. "Once it starts, you'd better be sure you're where you want to be, because odds are, you just may be there a while."

"Ma'am," he said, gathering a good eight to ten quartered logs in his strapping arms, adding them to the already healthier pile, "No offense, but I grew up in north Texas. I know all about freezing rain."

Of course, you do. But do you have any idea how well those Wranglers hug your—

"Mommy!" Ashley cried, skidding to a breathless stop alongside her. "Gramma said if you don't get in the house, you'll catch a death."

Gage chuckled.

The fact that he apparently not only found her, but

her entire family amusing, reminded Jess why she'd even tracked him down. To ask him to leave.

"Please tell Grandma I'll be right in," she said to her daughter, giving the pom-pom of her green crocheted hat an affectionate tweak.

"'Kay." As fast as her daughter had appeared, she ran off.

"She's a cutie," Gage said.

"Thanks."

"Hope I'm not overstepping—" he reached for another log "—but Doc told me what happened to your husband. Must've been a comfort having your girls."

More than you'll ever know.

Something about the warmth in the stranger's tone wrapped the simple truth of his words around her heart. Throat swelling with the full impact of a loss that suddenly seemed fresher than it had in a long time, she lacked the strength to speak.

"Anyway," he continued, "just wanted to say sorry. You got a raw deal."

Lips pursed, she nodded.

"You should..." he nodded to the house "...go in."

Though she couldn't begin to understand why, the fact that he cared if she was cold irritated her to no end. Here, she'd come over to tell him thanks, but no thanks, she and her girls could handle working this ranch just fine on their own, when in a span of fifteen minutes he'd managed to chop more wood than she had in a month. Now, just as Dwayne used to, he was protecting her. Sheltering her from the worst an Oklahoma winter could dish out. Coming from her husband, her high-school sweetheart, the only man she'd ever loved, the notion had been endearing. Coming from this stranger, it was insulting.

The truth of the matter was that in a few months, once she could no longer afford to pay him, he'd be gone. Just like her husband. Then, there she'd be, once again struggling to make a go of this place on her own. But that was okay. Because, stubborn as she was, she'd do just that.

Oh, Jess knew the stranger meant well, but the bottom line was that she was done depending on anyone for survival. And make no mistake, out here, eking a living from the land was a matter of day-to-day survival.

As a glowing bride, she'd still believed in Happily Ever Afters. She now knew better. Loved ones could be snatched from you in a black second. Twisters could take your home. Learning life doesn't come with a guarantee had been one of Jess's most valuable lessons. It had taught her to appreciate every day spent with her daughters and parents and existing few friends. It had also taught her not to let anyone else in. Even if that someone was only an apparently well-meaning hired hand. For the inevitable loss of his much-needed help would hurt her already broken spirit far more than long days of working the ranch hurt her weary muscles.

"Look," she finally said, all the more upset by the fact that the freezing rain had started, tinkling against the tin roof and the rusted antique tiller Dwayne had placed at the corner of the yard for decoration. They'd had such plans for this old place. Dreamed of bit by bit fixing it up. Board by board, restoring it to the kind of working outfit they'd both be proud of. "I'm not sure how to politely put this, so I'm just going to come right out and say it. You're, um, doing an amazing job with this wood, and there's no doubt I could always use an extra hand, but—"

"You don't want me here?"

"Well…" Jess didn't want to be rude to the man, but, yeah, she didn't want him here.

"Tell you what," he said, not pausing in his work. "Doc and my dad are pretty proud of themselves for hooking us up, and—"

Her cheeks flamed. "They *what?*"

"I didn't mean it like *that*," Gage said, casting her a slow and easy and entirely too handsome grin. "Just that I've needed a change of scenery and you've obviously needed a strong back. To a couple of coots like Doc and my old man, I suppose we must seem like a good pair."

"Oh. Sure." Now, Jess's cheeks turned fiery due to having taken Gage's innocent statement the wrong way.

"Back to what I was saying, how about I stay through the afternoon—just long enough to get you a nice stockpile of wood, then be on my way before the weather gets too bad? Doc won't even have to know I'm gone till I'm over the state line."

"You'd do that? Pretend to stay, for me?"

"Hell," he said with a chuckle, "if I'd stand out here all afternoon, chopping wood for you in the freezing cold, why wouldn't I do a little thing like leaving you on your own?"

His laughter was contagious, and for an instant,

Jess's load felt lightened. Only, curiously enough, her healthier woodpile had less to do with her improved mood than the warmth of Gage's smile.

* * * * *

Here's a sneak peek at
THE CEO'S CHRISTMAS PROPOSITION,
the first in USA TODAY *bestselling author*
Merline Lovelace's
HOLIDAYS ABROAD *trilogy,*
coming in November 2008.

American Devon McShay is about to get the
Christmas surprise of a lifetime when she meets
her new client, sexy billionaire Caleb Logan, for
the very first time.

Silhouette
Desire

Available November 2008

Her breath whistled out in a sigh of relief when he exited Customs. Devon recognized him right away from the newspaper and magazine articles her friend and partner Sabrina had looked up during her frantic prep work.

Caleb John Logan, Jr. Thirty-one. Six-two. With jet-black hair, laser-blue eyes and a linebacker's shoulders under his charcoal-gray cashmere overcoat. His jaw-dropping good looks didn't score him any points with Devon. She'd learned the hard way not to trust handsome heartbreakers like Cal Logan.

But he was a client. An important one. And she was willing to give someone who'd served a hitch in the marines before earning a B.S. from the University of Oregon, an MBA from Stanford and his first million at the ripe old age of twenty-six the benefit of the doubt.

Right up until he spotted the hot-pink pashmina, that is.

Devon knew the flash of color was more visible than the sign she held up with his name on it. So she wasn't surprised when Logan picked her out of the crowd and cut in her direction. She'd just plastered on her best businesswoman smile when he whipped an arm around her waist. The next moment she was sprawled against his cashmere-covered chest.

"Hello, brown eyes."

Swooping down, he covered her mouth with his.

Sheer astonishment kept Devon rooted to the spot for a few seconds while her mind whirled chaotically. Her first thought was that her client had downed a few too many drinks during the long light. Her second, that he'd mistaken the kind of escort and consulting services her company provided. Her third shoved everything else out of her head.

The man could kiss!

His mouth moved over hers with a skill that ignited sparks at a half-dozen flash points throughout her body. Devon hadn't experienced that kind of spontaneous combustion in a while. A *long* while.

The sparks were still popping when she pushed off his chest, only now they fueled a flush of anger.

"Do you always greet women you don't know with a lip-lock, Mr. Logan?"

A smile crinkled the skin at the corners of his eyes. "As a matter of fact, I don't. That was from Don."

"Huh?"

"He said he owed you one from New Year's Eve two years ago and made me promise to deliver it."

She stared up at him in total incomprehension. Logan hooked a brow and attempted to prompt a non-existent memory.

"He abandoned you at the Waldorf. Five minutes before midnight. To deliver twins."

"I don't have a clue who or what you're..."

Understanding burst like a water balloon.

"Wait a sec. Are you talking about Sabrina's old boyfriend? Your buddy, who's now an ob-gyn doc?"

It was Logan's turn to look startled. He recovered faster than Devon had, though. His smile widened into a rueful grin.

"I take it you're not Sabrina Russo."

"No, Mr. Logan, I am *not*."

* * * * *

Be sure to look for
THE CEO'S CHRISTMAS PROPOSITION
by Merline Lovelace.
Available in November 2008
wherever books are sold,
including most bookstores, supermarkets,
drugstores and discount stores.

Silhouette®

Romantic
SUSPENSE

**Sparked by Danger,
Fueled by Passion.**

Lindsay McKenna
Susan Grant

Mission: Christmas

Celebrate the holidays with a pair
of military heroines and their daring men
in two romantic, adventurous stories
from these bestselling authors.

Featuring:

"The Christmas Wild Bunch"
by *USA TODAY* bestselling author
Lindsay McKenna

and

"Snowbound with a Prince"
by *New York Times* bestselling author
Susan Grant

Available November wherever books are sold.

REQUEST YOUR FREE BOOKS!

2 FREE NOVELS PLUS 2
FREE GIFTS!

Love, Home & Happiness!

YES! Please send me 2 FREE Harlequin® American Romance® novels and my 2 FREE gifts (gifts are worth about $10). After receiving them, if I don't wish to receive any more books, I can return the shipping statement marked "cancel." If I don't cancel, I will receive 4 brand-new novels every month and be billed just $4.24 per book in the U.S. or $4.99 per book in Canada. That's a savings of close to 15% off the cover price! It's quite a bargain! Shipping and handling is just 25¢ per book, along with any applicable taxes.* I understand that accepting the 2 free books and gifts places me under no obligation to buy anything. I can always return a shipment and cancel at any time. Even if I never buy another book from Harlequin, the two free books and gifts are mine to keep forever.

154 HDN EEZK   354 HDN EEZV

Name	(PLEASE PRINT)	
Address		Apt. #
City	State/Prov.	Zip/Postal Code

Signature (if under 18, a parent or guardian must sign)

Mail to the **Harlequin Reader Service:**
IN U.S.A.: P.O. Box 1867, Buffalo, NY 14240-1867
IN CANADA: P.O. Box 609, Fort Erie, Ontario L2A 5X3

Not valid to current subscribers of Harlequin® American Romance® books.

Want to try two free books from another line?
Call 1-800-873-8635 or visit www.morefreebooks.com.

* Terms and prices subject to change without notice. N.Y. residents add applicable sales tax. Canadian residents will be charged applicable provincial taxes and GST. Offer not valid in Quebec. This offer is limited to one order per household. All orders subject to approval. Credit or debit balances in a customer's account(s) may be offset by any other outstanding balance owed by or to the customer. Please allow 4 to 6 weeks for delivery. Offer available while quantities last.

Your Privacy: Harlequin is committed to protecting your privacy. Our Privacy Policy is available online at www.eHarlequin.com or upon request from the Reader Service. From time to time we make our lists of customers available to reputable third parties who may have a product or service of interest to you. If you would prefer we not share your name and address, please check here. ☐

HAR08R2

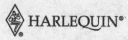

HARLEQUIN®

American ★ Romance®

LAURA MARIE ALTOM
A Daddy for Christmas

THE STATE OF PARENTHOOD

Single mom Jesse Cummings is struggling
to run her Oklahoma ranch and raise her
two little girls after the death of her husband.
Then on Christmas Eve, a miracle strolls onto
her land in the form of tall, handsome bull
rider Gage Moore. He doesn't plan on staying,
but in the season of miracles, anything
can happen....

**Available November
wherever books are sold.**

LOVE, HOME & HAPPINESS

www.eHarlequin.com   HAR75237

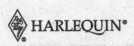

HARLEQUIN®
American ★ Romance®

COMING NEXT MONTH

#1233 A DADDY FOR CHRISTMAS by Laura Marie Altom
The State of Parenthood
Single mom Jesse Cummings is struggling to run her Oklahoma ranch and raise her two little girls. Then a miracle strolls onto her land in the form of a tall, handsome Texan. Gage Moore has his own troubles, so he doesn't plan on staying. But in the season of miracles, anything can happen....

#1234 THE CHRISTMAS COWBOY by Judy Christenberry
The Lazy L Ranch
Hank Ledbetter isn't the type of cowboy to settle down and raise a family. So when his grandfather orders him to give private riding lessons to Andrea Jacobs—a woman so *not* his type—he's bowled over by his attraction to the New York debutante. Andrea has another man in her life…but Hank's determined to be the only man kissing her this Christmas!

#1235 MISTLETOE BABY by Tanya Michaels
4 Seasons in Mistletoe
Rachel and David Waide want nothing more than to have a child. But after years of trying they are growing apart. Then Rachel discovers she is—at long last—pregnant! Now the two have to work their way back and remember all the love they used to share. Luckily, they'll receive a little help—in the form of a wedding, and the magic of Christmas.

#1236 THE COWBOY AND THE ANGEL by Marin Thomas
In his cowboy gear, Duke Dalton stands out in a crowd in downtown Detroit. He's there to set up his business, but some runaway kids are bunking in his warehouse. They need a Christmas angel—Renée Sweeney. And though Renée will do what she can to help the children, she wants nothing to do with Duke!

www.eHarlequin.com